Never, if he lived to be a hundred, would he understand women

Nikos swung his sleek, high-performance sports car into his parking space directly outside the pediatric emergency department. He'd offered her marriage and put a diamond the size of New York on her finger. And she'd given it back.

What was going on in her head? How many women had longed for him to make exactly that gesture? Her refusal had been genuine. And yet she still wanted him; he knew that. So why hadn't she just said yes?

Acknowledging that he didn't have any answers made him realize how little he knew about her. What, in all honesty, had they shared in the six passionate months they'd spent together? Sex, he acknowledged ruefully. They'd lived in a small, intimate bubble that had involved only their work at the hospital and the two of them. Nothing had intruded.

And that had been the way he'd wanted it.

Locking his car, Nikos strode purposefully toward the entrance of the pediatric emergency department, his naturally competitive nature roused by the block she'd erected in the path of their relationship.

She would marry him, he vowed silently. She was carrying his baby.

Dear Reader,

A few months ago I was stuck in traffic listening to the radio, absorbed by one young female caller describing how she found it impossible to commit to a relationship. Her ex-husband had hurt her so badly that she'd decided she was never going to put herself in a position where that could happen to her again.

And I was so sad for her. I kept thinking, what if she meets a man who could make her happy, but she's too afraid to take the chance? She'll miss out on a lifetime of love and happiness!

I started wondering what would make a person be willing to take that risk again, and by the time I arrived home I had a story to tell.

My heroine, Ella, won't allow herself to trust a man. Her childhood taught her to guard her feelings, and that's what she's done all her life—until the day she meets handsome Greek doctor Nikos Mariakos. Nikos is the doctor you would want on duty the night you take your sick child to the emergency room. He's dedicated, clever and confident, and soon Ella is in love. Yes, she even learns to trust.

But then she learns that Nikos has secrets—and those secrets rip their love into pieces and threaten their future together.

As I watched Ella battle her trust issues, one thing became very clear to me: the goal was worth fighting for. Yes, love can be a risk, but it is also the greatest gift.

With love,

Sarah
X

THE GREEK BILLIONAIRE'S LOVE-CHILD
Sarah Morgan

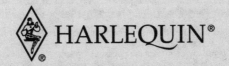

TORONTO • NEW YORK • LONDON
AMSTERDAM • PARIS • SYDNEY • HAMBURG
STOCKHOLM • ATHENS • TOKYO • MILAN • MADRID
PRAGUE • WARSAW • BUDAPEST • AUCKLAND

Recycling programs
for this product may
not exist in your area.

ISBN-13: 978-0-373-06687-2
ISBN-10:   0-373-06687-2

THE GREEK BILLIONAIRE'S LOVE-CHILD

First North American Publication 2009

Copyright © 2009 by Sarah Morgan

Printed in U.S.A.

Billionaire Doctors

Hot, jet-set docs at the top of their game—
professionally...and personally!

These desirable doctors are international playboys—
gorgeous Greeks, sexy sheikhs, irresistible Italians and
Australian tycoons.

Their playground might be the world of the rich and famous,
but their professional reputations are world renowned.

These billionaires dedicate themselves to saving lives by
day—and red-hot seduction by night....

PROLOGUE

It was a bad time to realise that she was in love.

The atmosphere in the resuscitation room was strained and tense—the child's injuries so severe that no one was holding out much hope of a good outcome.

No one, that was, except Dr Nikos Mariakos, the Greek consultant who had a reputation for making miracles happen.

Ella adjusted the oxygen flow with shaking hands and sneaked a glance at the man working across from her. Her heart tumbled, dipped and soared.

Why now? *And why this man?*

She'd broken both her rules.

Don't trust.

Don't love.

At the age of eight she'd learned that men were bad news and she'd locked away her emotions and thrown away the key.

But this man had not only found the key, he'd used it. And what had started as a scorching affair, *a physical release from the constant stress of working in the paediatric emergency department*, had turned into something deeper.

Ella felt a moment of pure panic, but the child's condition didn't allow time for reflection.

'Suction—more light.' He gave his orders in a calm,

detached tone, apparently undaunted by the enormous task that faced him. It was almost as if he relished the challenge. His hands didn't shake, his brow didn't sweat and there was no trace of emotion on his cold, handsome face as he worked to stabilise the critically injured child.

I really do love him, Ella thought helplessly, watching every movement of his swift, skilled fingers with something close to desperation. Only hours earlier they'd been in bed. Those same fingers had created a very different kind of magic and the sensual spell he'd woven had somehow unravelled the protective web she'd spun over years of suspicion and caution.

A feeling of dread seeped into her bones as she realised how vulnerable she was.

Love had punched holes through her defensive shield.

Love now made her open to the same agonising hurt she'd suffered as a child.

'Do you want to give him another unit of blood?' It was one of the more junior doctors who spoke, his face almost as pale as that of their small patient.

'No. I want to control the haemorrhage.' The consultant's coldly analytical approach to the critically injured child was in direct contrast to the less experienced doctor's agitation. 'Raise the temperature in here. I want overhead heaters and warming blankets.'

Ella quietly did as he instructed, remembering the day Nikos had started in the department. His reputation had caused such a stir that for days before his arrival no one had talked about anything but his technical brilliance and the fact that he was the youngest consultant ever appointed in the hospital.

And then he'd strode through the doors and the talk

from the females in the department had shifted from his clinical skills to the fact that he was sexy enough to start a riot in a nunnery.

Even Ella, with her natural suspicion of very handsome men, had been blinded. Not just by his startling good looks, but by his bold, determined approach to every case that came through the doors of the emergency department.

Dismissive of bureaucracy, Nikos Mariakos was fearless in his pursuit of clinical excellence. His willingness to challenge conventional thinking and push boundaries meant that he frequently clashed swords with the hospital management who were terrified by his indifference to protocol and policy.

Nikos didn't care.

When it came to his work, he cared about one thing alone.

His young patients.

It was as if he was on a one-man crusade to save every injured child.

And that included the little boy on the trolley.

'He's arrested. Get me a thoracotomy pack. I'm going to open his chest.'

A stunned silence greeted his statement and Phil, the anaesthetist, shook his head in disbelief. 'In the emergency department? You can't be serious, Nikos. Do you know the mortality rate for performing that procedure outside the operating room?'

Nikos was resuscitating the child. 'I'm sure you're about to remind me.'

The anaesthetist proceeded to do exactly that, but Nikos didn't pause in his efforts.

'Get that pack open, Ella,' he ordered. 'You should take a job with a medico legal company, Phil. They'd love you. Has someone called the cardiothoracic surgeons?'

'What the hell is the matter with you, Nikos? Were you dropped on your head as a child?' His colleague was perspiring under the heat of the lights, his concern for the patient eclipsed by concern for himself and the potential consequences of what the Greek consultant was proposing. 'Don't you ever follow protocol?'

'Not if following protocol means giving up on a child,' Nikos said coldly. 'This child has a penetrating chest wound which appears to be confined to the thorax. If I can stop the bleeding within the next few minutes, he stands a chance. Ella—the pack. Now.'

'Think of your reputation.' The anaesthetist became a shade paler as Nikos prepped the child's chest. 'You could be struck off.'

'If I'm struck off for doing my best for my patient then I would leave medicine happy. A bit like having a heart attack during sex.' Nikos spoke in a lazy drawl, nothing in his demeanour suggesting that he was about to perform major surgery. 'I've always thought that if you are going to make an exit, you should at least make it while striving for perfection.'

It must have been the impossible tension of the situation that made Ella want to laugh. Or perhaps it was just the inconceivable idea of someone with Nikos's physique and stamina dying during sex.

'Your girlfriend is obviously a lucky woman,' quipped one of the cheekier nurses, and Ella felt her face grow scarlet.

They'd always kept their relationship secret, but suddenly she had a wild desire to tell everyone that this incredibly talented man was *hers*. That she was the one he spent his nights with.

He'd chosen *her*.

His gaze met hers and her heart skipped several beats because she knew he'd read her mind.

A faint gleam of irony lit his dark eyes and then he held out his gloved hand.

'Scalpel,' he said softly, and she took a deep breath and handed him the instrument, feeling that the moment was almost symbolic. He had the ability to heal, but he also had the ability to hurt.

Would he hurt her?

The only thing she knew for sure was that if she were the one who was injured, he was the only doctor she would want in the room.

Unfortunately the anaesthetist didn't share her confidence. 'If you can make a joke then you have no idea of the seriousness of what you are about to do, Mariakos,' he said harshly, but Nikos was already operating.

'For this procedure to have any chance of success, it has to be performed within five minutes of cardiac arrest. I have four minutes remaining, Phil.' His tone was conversational. 'Do you want to talk or save a life?'

'I want you to consider what you're doing.'

'Retractor.'

Ella handed Nikos what he needed as sweat beaded on the anaesthetist's brow.

'The child will not survive if you do this, Nikos.'

'He won't survive if I don't do it.' Nikos worked swiftly and with cool precision, not once faltering as he carried out a procedure that would have been beyond the nerve or capability of most doctors. 'Now I see the problem.' He made it sound as though he was dealing with something routine. 'There's a tear in the atrium—give me a suture.'

Ella detached herself mentally from the emotional

side of the case. It was a procedure, not a child. If she thought about the human story behind every injury that came through the doors, she'd be an emotional wreck. So she passed the sterilised instruments, concentrating on what he was doing, trying to anticipate what he was going to need even though she'd never seen this performed before.

The anaesthetist wiped his forearm over his brow. 'If this child dies, the parents will sue you. Doesn't that frighten you?'

'I think you are frightened enough for both of us,' Nikos murmured, his fingers swift and skilled as he staunched the bleeding and repaired the damage. Cool, unflustered, he lifted his gaze to the monitor. 'Come on, *agori mou*. Fight for me. Put a little effort into this. So far I have been doing all the work. I am tired—it is your turn, I think.'

As they continued to resuscitate the child, Ella found that she was holding her breath.

If there was ever the slightest hope, Nikos never gave up. *Every child mattered to him.*

And, this time, his efforts were rewarded. The child's heart responded and the monitor flickered to life just as the cardiothoracic surgeon entered the room.

'You've missed the party.' Nikos didn't shift his focus from the child. 'How's he doing from your end, Phil?'

'Surprisingly well.' The anaesthetist sounded stunned. 'You're a cool customer, Mariakos. And you have the luck of the devil.'

'Is that why you're looking at me as if I've grown horns? I'm done here.' Nikos's gaze flickered to the cardiothoracic surgeon, who was watching with a faint smile of admiration. 'Do you want to close? I have no doubt you'll do a neater job than me. Sewing has never been my speciality. Do you have a bed on ITU?'

The cardiothoracic surgeon started to scrub. 'I'll arrange it. Are you sure you want me to finish off here?' His tone was dry. 'You seem to be doing very well by yourself.'

'I want to talk to the family.' Nikos stepped away from his patient and stripped off his gloves, allowing his colleague to take over. His eyes lingered on the monitor for a moment and then he nodded with satisfaction. 'If there's any change, call me.' And with that he strode out of the room.

His departure was greeted by stunned silence and then the junior doctor cleared his throat.

'When I grow up, I want to be him,' he muttered. 'What's his secret? I want to be that cool. Is it down to experience?'

'No, it's down to temperament.' The surgeon took over where Nikos had left off. 'You need two things to be a good cardiothoracic surgeon. Technical brilliance and balls of solid steel—no offence, ladies. Tell Mariakos that if he's ever bored with the emergency department, he can come and work with me.'

'I don't know about the rest of his anatomy, but the man has ice in his veins,' the anaesthetist snapped. 'And he's arrogant. Too sure of himself. If you ask me, he's going to come unstuck. Today, he was lucky.'

'I saw what he did, and it wasn't luck.' The cardiothoracic surgeon started to close the chest. 'It was skill. And I can't remember the last time I praised anyone other than myself so cherish the moment.'

'The child is alive.' Ella handed the surgeon the equipment he needed. 'And he's alive because Nikos was prepared to take a risk.'

'Maybe. But his lack of emotion worries me.' Phil adjusted the flow of gases. 'Technically he's brilliant, I agree. And, yes, he has…' he cleared his throat and re-phrased his colleague's earlier description '…*nerves* of steel. But he's cold. Doesn't that make you just a little uneasy?'

Ella kept her eyes down as she cleared away the remains of the pack, careful to give nothing away.

Yes, it made her uneasy.

It was easy to forget his emotional detachment when they were in bed. But out of bed…

She gave a little shake of her head, determined not to create problems that didn't exist.

Her own experiences as a child had given her a dysfunc-tional view of the world—she needed to remember that. She needed to remember that not every man was her father.

Phil stood up. 'It would be nice to see that he's human. Nice if that icy control of his slipped for five minutes. I'd like to think it was an act that he puts on when he's working— plenty of us do that in order to cope with the emotional stresses of this place. But Nikos Mariakos…' He shook his head. 'I don't think the man is blanking out his emotions. I don't think he has any. I don't think he's capable of feeling.'

Nikos paused outside the relatives' room, looking down at his shaking hands with wry self-mockery.

He didn't have to be back in the resuscitation room to know what they were saying about him.

Ice cold.

Emotionless.

All the usual things.

It was a good job they couldn't see him now or his rep-utation would be shattered into a million pieces.

Fortunately for his patients, his body had never betrayed him inside the resuscitation room. Only afterwards did the reaction come. *Only afterwards did the memories catch up with him.*

Nikos inhaled deeply, pushing aside the images that mocked him.

Images of a different child.

A child he hadn't been able to save.

But this time—this time he'd won the fight.

He pushed open the door and greeted the relatives, ignoring hospital protocol that demanded that he take a nurse in with him. Unlike many of his colleagues, Nikos didn't dodge the difficult task of handling emotional relatives. The thought of breaking bad news and then abandoning them to cry on a nurse was alien to him.

He was the one who had managed the case. He was the one who could answer their questions, although inevitably he never had an answer to the most desperate question of all.

Why?

Fortunately, on this occasion the news was better than anyone had hoped and ten minutes later he took refuge in his office, knowing that the staff would still be talking about the risks he'd taken.

He rolled his shoulders to relieve the tension and stared out of his office window to the busy city streets below. Thinking. Remembering…

'Nikos?'

Ella's voice came from the doorway and he turned, a smile on his lips because she was the one person who could relieve his current stress levels.

'Are you off duty?'

'Yes. The child is safely in ITU and doing well.' She strolled towards him, all long legs and sparkling eyes.

'Good.' But he wasn't thinking about the child.

She stopped in front of him and placed her fingers on his chest. 'You were amazing.'

'I thought Phil's heart was going to stop, along with the patient's.' Nikos was captivated by her sweet smile and her frank adoration. She was deliciously uncomplicated.

And she had a fabulous body.

'Phil is a very cautious person.'

Nikos pulled her into his arms, feeling the immediate response of his body as her softness pressed against him. 'You need cautious people in this business.'

'To counter people like you?' Her eyes teased him. 'You're not cautious, are you?'

'If you're asking if I know what I want, then the answer is yes.' Nikos lowered his head and took her mouth, tasting honey and temptation. 'At the moment what I want is you, in my bed, naked.'

'*My* bed.' She trailed a finger over his rough jaw, her breathing slightly faster than it had been before the kiss. 'We've only ever made love in my bed. It's been six months and we've never once been back to wherever it is you live. Do you realise that?'

Yes, he realised that.

'Your place is closer.' Smoothly he steered the conversation away from that particular topic. 'I'm hungry. What do I have to do to get some of your delicious cheese on toast?'

Her arms slid round his neck. Affection. Warmth. 'I would have thought you were sick of eating cheese on toast in my room. Are you sure you wouldn't rather go out to eat?'

'I want to have sex, then eat, then have sex again,' Nikos

purred, backing her against the wall and feeling the volcanic response of his body. 'And then have sex again. We'd get arrested for that in a restaurant.'

She was giggling, breathless—her eyes slightly shocked. 'Nikos, this is ridiculous. We always end up in my single bed in the nurses' accommodation. We've been together for six months. It's time to stop behaving like hormonal teenagers.'

Nikos brought his mouth down on hers, but his brain refused to be as easily distracted as his body.

Six months?

Surely that wasn't possible.

'Nikos?' She dragged her mouth away from his, laughter and love in her eyes.

Love?

Nikos stilled. When had that happened? *And why hadn't he noticed?*

Mentally, he retreated. 'I like sleeping in your single bed.' *She was getting too close.* He curved his hand over her bottom, knowing what had to be done, but finding it surprisingly difficult. Usually, ending a relationship was easy. 'You have a choice. Either I go for a ten-mile run or I take you to bed. Which is it to be?'

The sexual tension reached almost unbearable proportions.

'That's a tricky choice.' Her breathing was shallow. 'It isn't safe to be on the streets of London at this time of night.'

'Good decision.' Nikos kissed her again and reached for his jacket. As he urged her out of the door, he pondered on the best way to tell her that the relationship was over.

CHAPTER ONE

'I STILL can't believe he'd just dump you, Ella. Why would he do that?'

Ella stared straight at the long slender boat nestling quietly against the bank of the river, appalled by the discovery that her grip on her self-control wasn't as firm as she would have liked it to be. 'Obviously he didn't like me enough.' And even now, after four long months of no contact, she found it hard to believe that she wasn't going to see him again—*that the connection she'd thought was there hadn't existed for him.*

Helen made a disparaging noise. 'Ella, you told me he barely let you out of the bedroom for the six months you were together. He liked you.'

'He liked the sex.' Ella watched as a kingfisher dived into the water, a flash of iridescent green and blue, searching for breakfast. 'Men don't turn every sexual encounter into happy ever after, you know they don't. Women mate for life, men mate whenever the opportunity presents itself.'

But somehow she'd allowed herself to forget that fact.

She'd romanticised a relationship that had been based on physical chemistry and, worse than that, she'd trusted a man.

'Change the subject,' she said flatly. 'I need to just forget him and move on.' Which was what he'd done, wasn't it?

'How can you forget him? Ella, you're pregnant! What are you going to do?'

Ella clutched her tiny suitcase and stared at the long, slender canal boat. She'd learned a long time ago that if you focused hard enough, it was possible to hold back tears. So she stared. And gradually the flood levels of emotion subsided. The hot stinging in her throat became a dull ache and the pressure behind her eyes eased. It was OK. She was going to be OK. And so was the baby. She'd make sure of it.

'I'm going to stop crying over a man who doesn't deserve it. And while I'm deciding what to do about my life, I'm going to live in this place. I didn't know it was possible to live on a canal boat. I love it.'

The dark green paintwork gleamed in the sunshine and brightly coloured fresh flowers tumbled from boxes set along the low, flat roof. Ella leaped from the bank to the boat, landing on the polished wooden deck.

'Why did you pick this? You can't live in this isolated place.' Helen glanced nervously up and down the deserted path that ran alongside the sleepy, overgrown canal. 'You're a city girl. You like bright lights and people around you.'

'I want something different. I'm tired of that life.'

'Well, this is a bit extreme. When you said it was a canal boat, I thought it would be in a marina or something—not just moored in the middle of nowhere. You're going to have loads of weirdos wandering along here.'

'I like it.' Ella watched as a duck glided past, followed by her family of six fluffy ducklings. Her eyes misted. It wasn't all bad. *She was going to have a baby.* 'Aren't they sweet?'

'Yeah—if a nutter happens to come stalking you, they'll be the perfect weapon. You can pick one up and yell, "Duck."'

'Very funny. Are you coming aboard?'

'I don't know why you can't carry on living in my spare room.' Helen followed more cautiously onto the boat. 'I love having you.'

'I can't live with you for ever. I'll use this as a base while I decide what to do.' Ella unlocked the doors at the bow of the boat. 'It's so peaceful here.'

'Ella, you've been crying yourself to sleep for the past four months. You don't need peaceful!'

Without responding, Ella ducked down into the long, narrow sitting area. Dark green sofas were piled with contrasting cushions and the polished wooden floor gleamed in the sunlight. She could imagine herself curled up on the cushions in the bow of the boat, a cold drink in her hand.

Alone.

The sudden stab of pain took her by surprise and she dug her nails into her palms.

Alone was fine. Until she'd met Nikos, that had been her life choice.

And she wouldn't be alone for long, would she? Soon she'd have the baby. They'd be a family…

Helen was looking round doubtfully. 'Do you realise that we've only seen one other person since we arrived? And that was a man on his own, walking a dog. This is not a suitable place for a woman.'

Ignoring her, Ella wandered further down the boat, trying to be positive as she explored her new surroundings. 'The bedroom is cosy.' She dumped her suitcase on the floor. 'I'll unpack later.'

'Who did you say owns this place?'

'One of the consultants at the hospital—he's gone to

Australia for six months with his family. One of the conditions of living here is that I have to water the plants.'

'Ella, please…' Helen plopped onto the side of the bed. 'Just think about what you're doing.'

'I'm getting on with my life.' Ella knelt on the bed next to her and looked out of the window at the overhanging trees that brushed the still surface of the water. 'It's so calming here. I can wake up every morning gazing at that.'

'Crying. *Talk* to me, Ella. Tell me how you're feeling.' *Like he'd taken a scalpel to her heart.*

'I'm fine,' Ella said brightly. 'No morning sickness, no swollen ankles, no—'

'I'm not talking about the pregnancy—I'm talking about the way you feel inside. You shut everyone out, Ella. You always have.' Helen spread her hands in exasperation. 'Did you do it with him? Didn't you tell him how you felt?'

'He knew.' And that was why he'd ended it. For her, the relationship had been more than the hot sizzle of sexual attraction. He'd wanted shallow and she'd waded in deep. 'You want to know how I feel? I'll tell you. I feel as though I've been broken into a million tiny pieces. I've stuck the pieces back together and so far it's all holding, but I don't feel like me any more.'

'Is that why you're planning on living in the middle of nowhere?'

'I need space to work out what I want. And it's cosy here.' Ella looked out at the trees spilling over the path and listened to the mellow sound of ducks. 'I'll be all right. I'm a paediatric nurse—at least I already know how to pick up a baby and change a nappy.'

'I'm not worried about your ability to change a nappy.'
Helen swatted a fly. 'I just don't want you to be single.'

'There's nothing wrong with being single. Single can be
a lifestyle choice, you know. We single women earn our
own money, we buy our own homes, we—we…'

'We what? We have sex with ourselves? Hug ourselves
when we're miserable? Fix the car when the engine won't
start? Sounds great.' Helen recoiled as she noticed a spider
lurking in the corner. 'Sorry, I know it isn't politically
correct to admit it, but I'm not ready to turn into a spinster
yet and neither are you. Buried under all that insecurity,
you're an old-fashioned girl. The man made you pregnant.
You have to tell him about the baby.'

'No, I don't.' Strengthened by a core of steely determin-
ation, Ella lifted her chin. 'He didn't want me, Helen.'

And she would do everything she could to protect her
baby from the emotional agonies she'd suffered as a child.

'He didn't know you were pregnant. And you don't
know why he walked out.'

Oh, yes, she did. Ella closed her eyes. Shut out the
images. 'He had another life. A life he didn't tell me about.'

'That bit is bizarre, I agree.' Helen frowned. 'I still find
it hard to believe that the guy is *seriously* a billionaire. I've
never actually met a real live billionaire before.'

'And to think I used to make him cheese on toast.' Ella
slid off the bed and walked back through to the living area
of the boat. 'Must have been a real letdown after Michelin-
starred restaurants. No wonder he left. I was probably
giving him indigestion every night.'

Helen followed her. 'Perhaps not telling you about the
money was some sort of romantic test.'

'Stop endowing him with thoughtful, sensitive qualities.' Ella tugged open a cupboard and found plates and mugs. 'Nikos was a selfish, driven, work obsessed male who only wanted one thing.'

'Well, at least he was jolly good at that one thing.' Catching Ella's eye, Helen subsided with a shrug. 'Sorry— but I just don't see why the money would make him walk out. It doesn't make sense. God, this is frustrating. Don't you want to *talk* to him?'

'There's nothing to talk about. He lied to me and he left. He didn't even have the courage to tell me face to face— just sent me an email telling me that he was going back to Greece and that our relationship was over.'

Helen winced. 'I hate email. Did you ever reply?'

'No. Because that was the day I went to the doctor about being sick. Hard though it is to believe, it hadn't even occurred to me that I might be pregnant.' Ella rolled her eyes, embarrassed by her own stupidity. 'While I was in the waiting room I flicked through a celebrity magazine. And there was a four-page spread on Nikos.' Heart pounding, she broke off and pressed her fingers to her temples. She still couldn't actually believe it had happened to her.

Helen slipped her arms around her. 'I don't know what to say. I'm really sorry.'

'So am I,' Ella said wearily, extracting herself from the hug. 'But that's life, isn't it? I should be grateful that I found out what sort of man Nikos is before the relation-ship went too far. At least this way it's only me that gets hurt.' Better now, before the baby was born.

Funny how protective you could be about a person who hadn't even arrived in the world yet.

'But if he turned up, you'd talk to him, right?'

'He won't turn up.'

'How can you be so sure?'

Ella was silent for a moment. 'Because he's married.' Saying the words made her wince. She felt ashamed, even though she knew she had nothing to be ashamed of. *Another woman's man.* 'I suppose that's why he didn't want emotional attachment. He already has one. His wife's name is Ariadne. And she must have the tolerance of a saint to keep taking him back after all the affairs he's had. All the time he was in London, he had a wife back home in Greece.'

Realising that Helen hadn't actually responded to her confession, Ella turned and found her friend staring at her in appalled horror.

'Married?'

'Yes.' Ella gave a twisted smile. 'Don't look so shocked. I feel bad enough as it is.'

'How do you know he's married?'

'I've seen his wedding photos. They were plastered all over that same celebrity magazine that told me he was a billionaire. She's very pretty. They obviously got married very young.'

'Why didn't you tell me this before?'

'Why do you think? I despised myself for having an affair with a married man. I'm hardly going to boast about it, am I?'

'I'm your best friend! And I can't believe you're only telling me this now. The rat. Oh, Ella…' Helen sank down onto the sofa and drew in several panicky breaths. 'I—I wish you'd told me this before. If I'd known… Oh, my God, what have I done?'

'You haven't done anything. It's me who—' registering Helen's dramatic reaction, Ella frowned, puzzled. 'What are you talking about? What *have* you done?'

There was a long, painful silence while Helen just gazed at her, wide-eyed with guilt and trepidation. 'You have to understand that I had your best interests at heart…'

'Now you're making me nervous.' Ella felt a sinister tingling in her nerve endings and dread seeped through her veins as she watched her friend's face turn pale.

'I didn't know he was married. I thought the pair of you were just being stubborn and that you could work it out if you'd only get together.'

Ella stared at her, her heart pounding. 'Helen…'

'I wrote to him,' Helen confessed, her eyes glistening with tears. 'You're my best friend and I've been listening to you crying your heart out every night for four months. I was *furious* with him and I thought if he knew about the baby…'

'You *told* him about the baby?' Ella felt the colour drain from her cheeks. 'Helen, *no!*'

'I'm so sorry.' Helen was crying openly now, her hands over her face. 'It was the wrong thing to do. I see that now. But you can be so stubborn and so can he, and the two of you seemed *so* in love. I thought that if I could just get you together, you'd be able to sort it out. I thought I was helping—I wanted you to be happy…'

'What have you done?' Breathing like someone in the last stages of labour, Ella struggled to think straight. 'What if he comes? If you told him about the baby…'

'But perhaps it will be a good thing if he comes. You'll talk and—'

'Helen, he's a married man and as far as I'm concerned that's the end of it! A man can't have two families!' Saying the words was agony. 'How could you do this? How could you interfere with my life?' Distraught, Ella's voice cracked and Helen rubbed the tears from her own face.

'I didn't know he was married! You'll never forgive me, I know, and I wish I could turn the clock back. It's just that for your whole life you've been screwed up about men and I thought I was helping.'

'I know I'm screwed up about men!' Ella's voice was hoarse. 'I'm completely dysfunctional when it comes to men, I admit it. And I've been proved right, haven't I? He lied to me, Helen. He lied about his wife, about the fact he's a billionaire—all lies. I don't think he said a single honest thing to me. And no conversation is going to change that. That sort of deception is *not* an accident. And if he does walk through that door, the only thing he's going to get from me is a black eye.'

'Perhaps you'd better give me one, too. I deserve it.' Helen rummaged in her bag for a tissue and blew her nose. 'I hate to say this but we're due at the hospital. We're both on a late shift. Do you want to call in sick? The new paediatric emergency department will probably fall apart if you're not there, but I can make excuses.'

'No way.' Ella closed her eyes for a moment. She couldn't afford to lose her job. She had a baby to support. And, anyway, they needed her at the hospital. 'I'll be fine. Management have refused Rose's request for extra staff yet again and the place is so busy.'

'It's the hot weather.' Helen looked out of the window at the blue sky. 'The tourists will already be on the beach, hitting themselves with cricket bats and being stung by wasps.' She bit her lip and turned back to her friend. 'I'm sorry, El.'

'Forget it. It's done.' Numb with shock, her mind in a spin, Ella stared sightlessly out of the window. 'You go. I'll lock up here.'

Helen hesitated, clearly torn between going and staying. 'Ella…'

'Just go.'

He wouldn't come, Ella tried to reassured herself as she listened to the soothing lap of the water against the sides of the wooden boat and tried to stay calm. He was married. He probably already had children. She'd been a convenient distraction while he'd been in London, nothing more.

Greek or not, he wasn't going to care that she was pregnant.

It was over.

His emotions threatening to overwhelm him, Nikos glanced around the waiting room of the paediatric emergency department, aware that some sort of response was expected from him. Never before had it been this difficult to concentrate on work. His stress levels mounting with every second that passed, he dutifully scanned the neat rows of small red seats, the colourful play area and the bright murals that livened the walls. 'You have a separate entrance for the children?'

'Yes. From the moment they come through the main door, they're separated from the adults. What do you think?' Rose, the senior nurse in charge of the main emergency department, looked at him nervously. 'We've had builders working non-stop for the past four months.'

Trying to show an interest, Nikos strode through the cheerful reception area and paused in the doorway of one of the cubicles. As well as state-of-the art equipment, there were neat boxes of toys, piles of children's books and DVDs. 'Resuscitation room?'

'Next door on your left.' Rose hurried along next to

him, struggling to match her stride to his. 'Can I ask you something, Professor?' They were in the resuscitation room now and Nikos was mentally itemising each piece of equipment in an attempt to distract himself from the issue that had dominated his brain for the past week.

'Call me Nikos, and, yes. Ask.'

'We're thrilled you're here, obviously but—why did you take this job?' Rose gave an apologetic shrug. 'You're in demand all over the world. I heard you lecture two years ago. The auditorium was completely packed out—there wasn't even breathing room.'

'Perhaps it was raining outside,' Nikos drawled lightly, and Rose gave a lopsided smile.

'I think we both know that wasn't the case. You could be working anywhere. Why us?'

'Sick children are sick children. It doesn't matter what the setting is.' Nikos cast his eye over the intubation tray, refusing to reveal his real reason for being there, even though he knew it would become apparent soon enough. 'Tell me about the staff.' He kept his tone neutral. 'They are paediatric trained?'

'We have a core of staff who are paediatric trained and we also rotate staff from the main emergency department according to need. This afternoon the paediatric nurse in charge will be Ella. She's wonderful.'

Ella.

A hard knot of tension settled in his stomach and his brain was filled with a distracting image of perfectly smooth blonde hair, a sweet, seductive smile and curves designed to fuse a man's brain.

'I know Ella.' Not by a flicker of an eyelid to Nikos reveal just how well he knew her. 'We worked together in London.'

And now she was pregnant with his child.

A fact she'd concealed from him.

Sharp claws of anger dug into him like talons and he breathed deeply, searching for control, shocked by the raw intensity of his rage. Well aware that people called him the ice doctor, he wondered what they'd say if they knew that at the moment he was close to meltdown.

What was that phrase that people threw out so carelessly? *Everyone has their limit.*

Was this his?

Had he reached his limit?

With a supreme effort of will Nikos reminded himself that anger achieved nothing. Losing his temper was *not* going to help.

Emotion didn't solve problems. What was needed was rational discussion.

She was going to have her say. He was going to have his say.

It was all going to be calm and reasonable.

They were going to be civilised.

'You know Ella?' Rose was looking at him, surprised. 'That's wonderful.'

Nikos gave a cool smile, well aware that Ella was going to find the situation a great deal short of wonderful. *She'd kept the news of her pregnancy from him.* 'I'm looking forward to renewing our acquaintance.'

'Well, you won't have to wait long. She's on a late shift this afternoon. She'll be here any minute.'

As if on cue Nikos heard her laughter from somewhere behind him and the sound released his temper. How could she laugh?

What was funny about intentionally depriving a man of his child?

Emotion thickened until he could taste it, until he was ready to put his fist through something.

Rational discussion was no longer on his wish list.

He forgot calm and reasonable.

He forgot civilised.

As she walked through the door, his anger erupted with volcanic force.

Her arms were raised, her hands occupied scooping her shiny blonde hair into a ponytail, a pose that seemed to emphasise the air of vulnerability that surrounded her. And suddenly Nikos found himself thinking about all the times he'd kissed his way down her slender, creamy throat while she'd writhed and moaned his name in a desperate plea for satisfaction. He remembered how shy she'd been the first time, how hard he'd found it to believe that a woman of twenty-four had so little experience.

Looking at her now, it was like taking a punch full in the gut.

She was wearing a scrub suit covered in pictures of jungle animals and for a moment Nikos was distracted. With her cheerful smile and sense of fun, she'd always had a gift for turning the emergency department into somewhere a child was almost pleased to visit.

'Hello, Ella.'

She stopped instantly, the smile dying on her lips as she saw him standing there.

Her arms dropped to her sides and she turned so pale that Nikos took an involuntary step forwards, preparing to catch her if she crumpled to the floor. Her breathing was audible and she stepped back, as if his approach represented a physical threat. For a moment she just stood there, her chest rising and falling as she sucked in air and stared at him.

Guilt, he thought grimly, as he watched her face. What she'd done was unforgivable and she knew it. But even as the anger took him by the throat once again, his hands were ready to catch her if she fell. There was no way he was going to let her land on the floor in a heap, pregnant with his child.

His lips burned with the need to speak his mind, but it wasn't the time or the place so instead Nikos communicated the full force of his anger in a single, hotly charged glance.

Apparently unaware of the dangerous shift in the atmosphere, Rose was cheerful. 'Ella—good timing. I had no idea that you and Professor Mariakos know each other. I'm delighted. It will make things so much easier. Now I have an experienced team running the paediatric emergency unit. It's going to be a happy summer.'

Anticipating anything but a happy summer, Nikos kept his simmering, accusing gaze fixed on Ella's pale, shocked face. 'It will be like old times.'

Something flickered in her slanting green eyes and he knew that she was thinking what he was thinking—that it was going to be *nothing* like old times.

This time when they worked there would be no intimate glances, no delicious thrill of excitement as they anticipated the time when they could be alone. No soft whispers, no swift smiles and absolutely no explosive sexual chemistry.

Only anger, blame and recrimination.

She'd hidden the fact that she was pregnant, and no woman was doing that to him again.

This time he wanted the right to be a father to his child.

Pain thumped through his gut and suddenly he wanted to tower over her and demand an explanation right here, right now. He wanted to know why the hell she hadn't contacted him herself.

The depth of his disillusionment surprised him because he'd always considered himself to be realistic about women.

Rose glanced between them. 'I've scheduled the two of you to work together on every shift right through the summer. I don't need to tell you that the hospital management are scrutinising this department very closely. I know it's going to be a fantastic success.'

Nikos dragged his gaze from Ella's but somehow his eyes simply shifted to a different part of her, this time her abdomen. To the untrained eye her pregnancy wasn't visible under the loose fabric of her scrub suit and yet he knew her so intimately that he could see the changes in her. Her glorious breasts were even fuller than usual, her hips more generously curved.

Cradling his child.

What would she have to say for herself?

What excuse would she give?

Was she one of these modern feminist women who wanted a baby but not a man?

His mouth tightened into a grim line as he pondered that possibility. If that was the case then she'd picked the wrong guy for a stunt like that. He was Greek. And she was about to discover exactly what that meant.

'Just breathe normally, sweetheart,' Ella soothed, her hand gently stroking the little girl's head as she tried to relax the terrified child. 'This mask is going to help you breathe.'

The little girl squirmed and clawed at the oxygen mask and Ella felt her heart contract as she tried to calm her. The poor child was terrified and her fear was making her condition worse.

Faced with a potentially life-threatening situation, Ella

pushed her own problems to the back of her mind and concentrated on the job she was trained to do.

Moments after Rose had given her the keys to the drug cupboard, the department had suddenly been swamped with patients. A dog bite, two asthma attacks and a child who had slipped while scrambling over the cliffs and sustained a nasty laceration to his lower leg.

Denied any opportunity to dwell on the implications of Nikos's presence, Ella had taken the most serious of the cases, a three-year-old girl with an acute asthma attack.

Thank goodness for training, she thought numbly as she adjusted the flow of oxygen and carefully observed the child's breathing. It was only training that was allowing her to function as if nothing was wrong. Her hands were doing the right things and her mouth was saying the right things, but inside she was shocked and shaking.

After Helen's confession, she'd cycled the brief distance along the canal to the hospital, her mind sifting through the various scenarios and how she'd handle them.

He'd come. Deep down, she'd known he'd come. And she'd decided that the most important thing was to stay calm and not allow emotion to play a part in their discussion. She'd be dignified and distant and keep the conversation focused on facts and nothing more. She'd find out what he wanted in terms of access and then go away and think about it. Nothing personal. She'd dismiss him as easily as he'd dismissed her.

At least, that had been the theory.

But how could any woman dismiss a man like Nikos Mariakos? How did you dismiss six feet two inches of strikingly good-looking, unwaveringly confident, muscle-packed male? Muscle-packed *angry* male.

Fortunately he'd gone with Rose to complete some paperwork, leaving Ella to work with Alan, a doctor with six months' accident and emergency experience who was spending the next month in the paediatric department as part of his training. Alan was unfailingly polite and courteous and perfectly competent with the routine stuff that came through the doors of the main emergency department. Privately, Ella wasn't sure he had the skill set to work with sick children, but she was hoping she'd be proved wrong.

So far three-year-old Tamsin had refused to allow him to listen to her chest, and nothing he tried could persuade her to co-operate. Flustered and out of his depth, the young doctor grew red in the face as he tried to reason with the child using a falsely bright voice.

Sensing his lack of confidence in a way that children always seemed able to do, Tamsin's panic increased and she flailed her little arms, becoming more and more upset and making it harder for Ella to calm her.

'Sweetheart, he's not going to hurt you.' Deciding that his presence was counter-productive, she discreetly waved a flustered Alan away from the trolley and picked up a doll from the toy box. 'This is Angie, isn't she beautiful? We're going to put a dress on her and then give her some special air to breathe, just like you. Which dress do you think? You choose.' She grabbed two dresses from the box and held them up. 'Pink or purple?'

Tamsin was panting for breath but she stopped clawing at the mask and pointed to a dress.

'Pink? Good choice. I love pink, too.' Ella pulled the pink dress over the doll's head and Tamsin reached out a hand for the doll.

'Say please, Tams,' the child's mother muttered, but

Ella didn't care about manners. She just wanted the child to keep the oxygen mask on.

'Are you going to help me put a mask on Angie? Oops— it's a bit big.'

Forgetting her own mask, Tamsin tried to help the doll.

'Good girl. Aren't you clever? She'll soon be feeling all better.' As Ella praised the child she glanced at the monitor again and felt a flash of unease. Worried about what she was seeing, she glanced at the child's mother. 'Amanda, has she had an attack like this before?'

'Nothing this severe.' The woman was cradling a young baby and trying to calm Tamsin at the same time. 'Just breathe through the mask like the nurse is telling you, Tams.'

'Has she had a cold? Any sort of infection you're aware of?'

'Nothing.' The baby started to cry and Amanda shifted the tiny bundle onto her shoulder with an apologetic look. 'Sorry. I wouldn't have brought the baby but I didn't have anyone to leave her with. Shh, Poppy—not now. Good girl, hush.'

Alan pushed his glasses higher up his nose. 'Someone could give your husband a ring, if that would help?'

Amanda gave a quick shake of her head and looked anxiously at Tamsin, clearly afraid of upsetting her still more. 'He's not on the scene any more,' she murmured quietly. 'Not since he discovered I was having this one.'

Ella felt a rush of sadness as she focused on Tamsin's sweet face. Long eyelashes. Blonde curls. And no father.

Another fractured family.

He should be here, she thought grimly, *holding his little girl when she needed him.*

Mortified at having been tactless, Alan mumbled an

apology, but Ella was too concerned about the condition of the little girl to dwell on the unreliability of the male gender.

'Alan, that salbutamol inhaler isn't having much of an effect. Do you want to give her some prednisolone?'

'She doesn't seem to be wheezing that badly.' Wary of approaching the child and unsettling her again, Alan hovered a safe distance from the trolley. 'Perhaps we ought to just try checking her peak flow?'

'She won't be able to manage it. She's too young.' Ella contemplated telling him that wheeze didn't give an accurate indication of airway obstruction, but decided it would be better to mention it later when they were alone. She didn't want to worry the child or the mother.

Suddenly she wished that Nikos hadn't chosen that moment to disappear with Ruth. It was impossible not to compare Alan's hesitant, hyper-conservative style with Nikos's bold, fearless approach to every emergency that crossed his path. He might be the last man in the world she wanted to see personally, but professionally he was a dream.

She was swiftly weighing up her options when Tamsin's small hand slid into hers. She looked exhausted and frightened, but the trust in her eyes tugged at Ella's heart.

'You're going to be fine, sweetheart. We'll make you better.' Her hand tightening over the child's, Ella looked at Alan. 'She needs prednisolone.' She spoke firmly, hoping that Alan would realise that she had experience in this area and just agree with her. 'I think a dose of 20 milligrams would be a good idea.'

Alan rubbed a hand over the back of his neck. 'I'm wondering whether perhaps I might just pick the prof's brains on this one.'

Ella gritted her teeth. 'Go ahead.' She didn't really care, just as long as someone with more experience than Alan checked the little girl. 'See if he's free.' *Do it now.*

As if the cosmos had ordered it, Nikos strode into the room at that moment. He'd shed his jacket, rolled his shirt-sleeves up to the elbows and everything about him was relaxed and confident. 'Everything all right in here?'

'Professor...' Alan straightened, a flicker of awe in his eyes. 'We weren't sure whether or not to go straight ahead and give her a dose of prednisolone or wait a bit and see if the inhalation improves her breathing. It's been a bit tricky, persuading her to co-operate.'

Nikos took one look at the gasping child and murmured, 'Give the prednisolone—now,' in a tone that suggested the question should never have been asked.

Alan gave Ella an apologetic look and she gently pulled her hand from Tamsin's. 'I'm not going anywhere,' she soothed as the child gave a whimper of protest and clutched at the air. 'I'm right here. Just getting you something to help you breathe.'

She felt Nikos's gaze on her as she reached for the dose she'd already prepared in anticipation of that exact outcome.

'Her sats are 95 percent.' Ella turned back to the child, making encouraging noises as she coaxed the medicine down the little girl, painfully conscious of Nikos's powerful frame on the other side of the trolley. 'The charts are behind you if you want to take a look.'

But Nikos didn't look at the charts. He was looking at his little patient.

'Tamsin?' A smile danced in his eyes and his expression changed from detached to playful. 'You have no idea how happy I am to see you.'

Tamsin shrank closer to Ella, like a tortoise retreating into the safety of its shell to hide from danger. 'Go away.'

Nikos leaned on the trolley to reduce his height and make himself less intimidating. 'I will if you want me to, but first I was hoping if you could help me out with this. I have no idea what to do with it.' From his pocket he produced a small stuffed mermaid with long golden hair. Despite her growing stress levels Ella couldn't help smiling because it was so typical of him to know exactly how to relate to each patient.

People said he was cold, but she knew that wasn't always the case.

The little girl's expression changed from panic to interest. Still clutching Ella's hand, she reached out for the toy, but Nikos held it just out of reach. 'First you have to give her a name. What are we going to call her?'

Ella caught the startled expression on Alan's face and knew that he was wondering why a professor of international repute would choose this moment to play mermaids with a little girl.

He looked at Nikos and saw him playing a frivolous game.

But Ella saw something very different.

She saw a skilled doctor using a distraction technique as a tool to give him answers. She saw Nikos's gaze rest on the child's chest as he assessed her breathing. She saw him encouraging the child to speak to him, so that he could evaluate how breathless she was.

And she saw a more relaxed child.

Look and learn, Alan, she thought wryly.

Nikos removed his stethoscope from his pocket. Tamsin immediately tensed and opened her mouth to protest loudly, but Nikos simply smiled and listened to the mermaid's chest, a look of total concentration on his handsome face.

'Well?' Playing along, Ella asked the question with a solemn expression on her face. 'How's the mermaid?'

Nikos nodded slowly. 'I think she might have swallowed some sea water but, other than that, she is good.'

Tamsin grabbed at the stethoscope. 'Me.'

'You want a turn?' Ella stroked Tamsin's silken curls. 'Would you like to listen?' She took Nikos's stethoscope and pretended to put it to the child's ears.

Seeing Ella smiling at Nikos, Tamsin started to relax. And Nikos was so skilful at dealing with her that by the time he finally placed the stethoscope on the child's chest, the little girl was so fascinated by him that she simply reached up a chubby hand and tugged at his dark hair. Then she pushed the mermaid in front of him again and Nikos smiled.

'She's all yours, *koritsi mou*. Make sure you look after her.'

Ella felt her heart flip because this side of him always left her in a puddle. She'd seen him verbally dissect experienced doctors who had fallen short of his expectations, she knew he was capable of being ruthless when the need arose, and yet with a small child he was a pussy cat—extraordinarily gentle, all that latent strength and power firmly leashed.

It was so hard to hate this man. So hard.

Choked by the thought of what could have been, she concentrated her attention on the monitor.

'Her sats are improving.'

Nikos nodded. 'She's doing fine.'

Despite the simmering tension between them, they worked together seamlessly, their movements smooth and slick as they did what needed to be done—a veneer of normality covering dangerous undercurrents…

Twice his fingers brushed against hers and in the end Ella stepped back from the trolley because although he was clearly indifferent to her, she didn't think she had the control to be this close to him and not react. He registered her retreat with a faint narrowing of his eyes and she wished she knew what he was thinking.

Why was he so angry?

He should have been thanking her for making things easy for him.

For quietly accepting his cold email brush-off.

She studied his handsome face for signs of strain— some evidence that the separation of the last four months might have affected him in the same way that it had affected her. Had he lost weight? Did he look as though he'd suffered?

But his face showed no sign of the ravages of worry. He looked strong and healthy, as if the weaknesses that permeated other mortals were afraid to lay a hand on him. The collar of his white shirt was undone and for a moment Ella's gaze lingered on the strong column of his throat, remembering how many times she'd pressed her mouth to that exact place. And his skin was a deeper bronze than usual, suggesting exposure to a more generous climate than that enjoyed by the South of England. Which reminded her of just one thing.

He'd been back in Greece.

With his beautiful Greek wife?

The pain almost split her in two and with the pain came anger.

He'd betrayed her and she needed to remember that. What she didn't need was to be seduced all over again by his skills as a doctor.

'So—her breathing is much improved.' Having won the child's confidence, Nikos addressed his remark to the little girl's mother. 'We need to try and establish what might have caused this attack. Her asthma is usually well managed?'

Still jiggling the baby in her arms, the woman nodded. 'Yes. In the winter she sometimes has problems if she has a chest infection, but nothing like this. We've rented a house on the coast with my sister and her family. One minute she was playing happily, the next she couldn't breathe.'

'And she is well at the moment? No cold? No temperature?' As he questioned the mother Nikos carried on examining Tamsin, this time checking her throat and her ears, feeling her glands and doing the same with the mermaid whenever required to do so by the little girl. 'Nothing different?'

Ella's heart jerked as her eyes settled on his skilled, bronzed fingers. *Fingers that could save a life or drive a woman crazy.*

She had so many questions.

Why was a billionaire playing at being a doctor?

Why hadn't he told her the truth about himself?

The mother was trying to give him the answers he wanted. 'I can't think of anything. She hasn't even been on the beach much because the children have mostly been playing in the house with the puppy.'

Nikos raised an eyebrow. 'Puppy?'

'I'm on holiday with my sister. They bought a puppy last week. A little spaniel. Tamsin loves the dog. They've been sleeping together.'

Ella exchanged a brief glance with Nikos just as the little girl snatched the mask off her face.

'Want to see Bruno.'

'Keep the mask on, Tams. Oh, my goodness.' Her mother was staring at Nikos. 'You think it might be the dog? Some sort of allergy? I hadn't thought of that.'

'It's possible.' Nikos reached for the notes. 'For the rest of the holiday play with the dog outside, not inside. When you get home, go and see your own doctor and talk it through with him. He might want to rethink your management plan.'

'Do you want to do a chest X-ray?' Ella asked. 'Shall I phone the radiographer?'

Nikos shook his head. 'Her oxygen saturation is improving, her heart rate has come down and her breathing has improved. I'm happy with that. You can move her to one of the cubicles and she can play for a while. If she's all right in an hour, she can go home.'

'I wish my sister would pick up my message and call. They've all gone for a walk.' Tamsin's mother fretted as the baby's wails grew louder. 'I want her to take the baby so that I can give Tams some attention.'

'The baby is probably picking up on your stress levels.' Ella held out her arms. 'Give her to me for a moment. I'll hold her while you give Tamsin a cuddle.' She took the baby, her heart melting as she studied the child's miniature features. If she felt like this about a stranger's baby, how would she feel about her own? 'There, now, Poppy. I bet you're wondering what you're doing in this strange place.' She murmured nonsense to the baby who promptly stopped crying and stared up at Ella.

Holding the baby securely, Ella smiled at her.

Apparently reassured and intrigued by a new face, the baby smiled back.

'She smiled!' Her arm around Tamsin and the mermaid,

Amanda laughed with amazement and delight. 'Did you see that, Tams? Poppy smiled at Ella. It's the first time. She was six weeks yesterday and we've all been trying to get her to smile. You've obviously got the touch. Do you have kids of your own?'

Ella's eyes shifted from the baby to Nikos and found him looking at her with an almost fierce intensity. The emotion inside her tumbled and threatened to spill over.

'No,' she said huskily, dragging her gaze from his before she made a fool of herself. 'I don't have children.'

'Oh, well, plenty of time.' Amanda stroked her daughter's hair. 'First you have to find that prince, don't you, Tams?' There was a wistful note in her voice that said her own 'prince' had fallen far short of expectations and Ella frowned slightly, wondering whether it was a good thing to fill a child's head with fairy stories.

If she had a little girl, she wouldn't do that, she vowed silently. She'd bring her up to have realistic expectations of life.

No relying on fictitious princes for happiness.

Without looking at Nikos, she handed the cooing, contented baby back to Amanda and, at that moment, another nurse popped her head in with an urgent request for him to look at another sick child.

With a smile at Tamsin and a fulminating look at Ella that promised a future far more complicated than that of any fairy story, he left the cubicle.

Ella felt a flicker of panic as she transferred Tamsin into one of the cubicles and contemplated the inevitable confrontation. What was he going to say to her? What excuses would he give? Was he going to tell her that his wife didn't understand him? That their marriage was in name only?

Frustrated with herself, she fished a book out off the shelf and sat down next to Tamsin. Nikos was married. The exact circumstances of that marriage were irrelevant. All that was between them was recriminations. And, on her part, self-blame.

Would he apologise for not telling her the truth?

Or was he one of those men who thought affairs were a natural part of marriage?

Forcing herself to concentrate, she read to Tamsin for a bit and then let her play with toys.

An hour later Nikos reappeared and pronounced her well enough to be discharged.

'Thanks so much for everything.' Amanda held Poppy against her shoulder with one hand, while Tamsin tugged at the other. 'You've been so great. Thank you.'

Nikos was writing up the notes as Tamsin dropped her mother's hand and held out her arms to Ella.

'Play.'

'No more playing today. You're going home, Tamsin.' Ella dropped into a crouch and smiled at her new friend. 'And you're going to have a lovely holiday.'

'You come.' Tamsin grabbed Ella's hand and gave her a tug.

Ella laughed and stood up. 'Now, that's a tempting in-vitation.' The way she felt at the moment she'd do anything to escape from the prospect of working with Nikos. 'Unfortunately, I can't come home with you.'

'I wish you could,' Amanda breathed. 'You're a miracle with the children. You have a real way about you.'

Ella saw Nikos's pen still and wondered what he was thinking.

Did he feel regret that they could never be a proper family?

Guilt that his child would grow up without a father?

Pushing that thought aside, she guided Amanda and the children out of the department and then reluctantly returned to the cubicle.

Fortunately there was no sign of Nikos and Ella felt a rush of relief as she cleared and restocked the room ready for the next patient.

The tension had formed a knot inside her stomach and she reminded herself that he wasn't going to say anything while they were at work.

Having used that fact to calm herself, she turned to leave the room only to find Nikos blocking her exit, his legs spread apart in a confrontational stance, the look in his black eyes dark and dangerous.

This time there was no evidence of gentleness or kindness. This wasn't a man who would be pulling a mermaid out of his pocket.

Anger surrounded him like a forcefield.

Closing the door firmly behind him, he strolled forward until his body was brushing against hers. 'It's time you and I had a conversation, *agape mou*.'

CHAPTER TWO

'I DON'T have anything to say to you, Nikos.' Heart racing, desperately flustered, Ella pushed at his shoulders but he didn't budge.

This wasn't a man about to apologise for anything. Mouth grim, he backed her against the wall and planted an arm either side of her shoulders, imprisoning her and blocking her escape. Through the fabric of his shirt she could feel the heat and power of his body and the immediate response of hers, and it appalled her that she could still feel like this after the casual, careless way he'd treated her.

He didn't care and yet still she couldn't switch off the screaming need inside her.

Her body was no judge of character, she thought bitterly, turning her eyes away from his in the hope of reducing temptation. He was everything male, from the top of his glossy dark head, down six feet four inches of supremely fit body, to the arrogant way he stood in front of her, as if he owned the world.

Which apparently he did, she thought, biting back a hysterical laugh as she remembered all the things she'd learned about him during that one, awful afternoon four months ago.

'You don't have anything to say to me? You are pregnant

with my child and you don't think you have anything to say to me?' His voice shook with emotion, his eyes narrowed to dangerous slits as he focused on her face. 'Answer me one question—were you going to tell me? If your friend Helen hadn't written that letter, *would you have told me*?'

'Why would you even care?'

The hiss of his breath was the only sound in the room. 'You are seriously asking me that question?'

She pushed at his chest, the enormity of the issue closing in on her like huge brick walls. 'We can't talk about this here. It's going to have to wait until we've finished work.'

He laughed, but the sound was bitter and contemptuous. 'I'm not letting you out of my sight, *agape mou*. And this is as good a place to talk as any. At the moment we have no patients. And I repeat—were you going to tell me?'

'I don't know!' Shaking now, Ella lifted her hands to her cheeks. 'You want an honest answer? *I don't know*. It was the hardest decision I've ever had to make.'

His mouth tightened into a grim line. 'I fail to see what is hard about telling a man that he is going to be a father.'

'It's hard when that man is already married!' Her passionate outburst was greeted by frozen silence.

It was as if she'd shot him at close range.

Nikos's sinfully handsome face grew several shades paler and his breathing became decidedly unsteady. 'What possible grounds do you have for making a statement like that?' His voice was hoarse and she shook her head, wondering why she suddenly felt guilty when it was his behaviour that had driven her away.

'I found out everything, Nikos.' It was hard to get the

words past the lump in her throat. 'Everything that you were hiding from me.'

His sudden stillness was marked. 'What,' he demanded in a thickened tone, 'was I supposed to be hiding?'

'Your secret life—the fact that you're a billionaire, with a wife waiting for you back in Greece.'

The silence that greeted her statement was like the strike of a blade through her heart. For months she'd nurtured a secret hope that she'd got it all wrong. She'd wanted desperately to be wrong, even though the evidence was damning. Even now, she was hoping for a denial.

But no denial was forthcoming.

Before that moment she hadn't realised that a silence could say so much.

He looked down at her, the shimmer of his eyes a warning of danger. 'This is the reason you didn't tell me about the baby? Because of some rumour you heard?'

'It wasn't a rumour.'

'Did you hear it from me? Did you hear from my lips that I have a wife?'

'You know I didn't.'

'And you didn't think it was worth asking me about this "secret life" of mine before you decided to deprive me of my child?'

'You walked out on me, Nikos! How could I ask you?'

'I did *not* know you were pregnant.'

The temperature between them was rising, the atmosphere so highly charged that Ella half expected the smoke detectors to be activated at any moment.

'What difference would it have made? You're married.' Reminding herself of that fact, Ella pushed at his chest and then wished she hadn't because touching him was sweet torture. She let her hands drop. 'I understand why you left me.'

'You understand nothing.' His voice held a harsh, brutal note. 'Nothing.'

She lifted her chin. Looked at him. Faced her mistake. 'I know that you lied to me. Maybe you're miserable together—I don't know—but that's no excuse. Whatever the state of your marriage, I can't be with a man I don't trust. That's the end of it for me.'

'Trust?' His laugh had a cynical edge to it. 'You dare talk to me about trust when you would have hidden your pregnancy from me?'

Feeling the fury in him, Ella felt a burst of frustration because the conversation was focused on him. *His* feelings. *His* ego.

He was thinking only of himself.

Had he once asked how she felt? Had he asked what had happened to her after he'd left? Did he care? No. He just cared that she hadn't told him she was pregnant.

Somehow he was twisting this whole thing to make it seem like her fault. She'd been expecting some sort of apology. Instead he was attacking her as if she'd committed a crime. 'The baby isn't the issue here, Nikos.'

'Why? Isn't it mine?' His tone was harsh and Ella gave a soft gasp of shock and lifted her hand.

The sound of the slap echoed around the room, the pain in her heart as great as the sting in her palm. 'How *dare* you? How dare you say that to me?'

'*Theos mou...*' Nikos lifted a hand to his cheek, incredulous dark eyes sweeping her face. 'It was a reasonable question.'

'It was not a reasonable question! It was a *totally of-*

fensive question!' She almost choked on the words. 'Especially coming from you. You lay in my bed night after night and made love to me and all the time you were married. What's your excuse? Your rampant sex drive? You have no idea how much I wish this wasn't your baby, Nikos! I would give anything for this not to be your baby.' Her hand still stung from the blow and part of her was embarrassed at her loss of control. It was to his credit that he hadn't returned the blow, she thought grudgingly, hating herself for not being able to maintain a front of cool indifference. 'No, I didn't tell you about the baby. I didn't want to do that to your wife!' Ella lifted her chin, pride giving her wobbly limbs the strength they needed, and her eyes clashed with his. 'And I didn't want to do that to my baby.'

'Our baby,' he corrected her in a driven tone, so angry that he was literally pulsing with it. She saw the flicker in his hard jaw and the flex of muscle in his wide, powerful shoulders. 'It's *our* baby.'

'A moment ago you were debating whether it was yours.' Sarcasm tasted bitter in her mouth. 'There is no "our", Nikos. Go back to your wife. Fix your marriage. We're finished.' Suddenly she felt drained and exhausted, the spirit sapped from her by the explosive force of the confrontation.

'Finished?' His tone was thickened, his dark eyes glittering with anger, a red streak on his cheek where she'd slapped him. 'We haven't even started. But you're right— we can't do this here. The way I feel at the moment, I'm not safe to be alone with you. I'll let you know when I'm ready to finish the conversation.'

Watching him stride away from her, Ella felt as though her heart was going to stop beating. Even though she knew it was foolish, a tiny part of her had desperately hoped he might just drag her into his arms and tell her that it was all a terrible mistake—that he loved her. That his wife didn't exist.

That she'd got it all wrong.

But that sort of thing didn't happen in real life, did it?

Humans were flawed, she reminded herself, restocking the resuscitation room on automatic. Endings weren't happy. Fairy-tales were for innocent children.

And true love was a myth.

Her emotions in pieces, Ella stumbled through the next few hours of her shift. Upset and distracted, her hands were shaking and she was unusually clumsy.

'That will have to be thrown away.' Nikos frowned impatiently as Ella dropped another instrument on the floor. 'What is the matter with you?'

You're the matter with me, Ella wanted to shriek, but instead she quietly disposed of the instrument, washed her hands and opened a fresh suture pack.

Her cheeks burned hot with humiliation.

The emergency department was the one area of her life where she considered herself confident, and now she was even messing that up.

She'd lost it.

In contrast, the crackling tension between them didn't appear to have affected the quality of Nikos's work in any way. As usual, he was ice cool, suturing the child's wound with hands that were entirely steady, maintaining a steady flow of conversation that involved fairies, palaces and magic kingdoms.

As if only hours earlier he hadn't been ready to remove Ella's head.

Envying his ability to detach himself from his problems, Ella tried not to mind that he obviously wasn't finding it remotely awkward working alongside her.

And that said everything about their relationship, didn't it?

He just didn't care enough. It wasn't hard for him whereas for her it was agony.

Not only had she been heartbroken by the end of their relationship, she now had the threat of further confrontation hovering over her like a stormcloud. He'd said that he couldn't talk about it yet.

Well, when? And where?

Trying to divert her mind, she kept her eyes fixed on either the patient or the instruments. But she was a nervous wreck. At one point Nikos made an exasperated sound and actually put his hand over hers to steady it. Ella immediately dropped what she was holding.

'Theos mou!'

'Sorry. I'm sorry,' she muttered, rapidly coming to the conclusion that the hospital wasn't going to be able to afford to keep her on at this rate.

Nikos dragged his impatient gaze from her flushed face and deftly tied the final stitch with fingers that were sickeningly steady.

'Those stitches can come out in ten days. I'm done here—well done, *koritsi mou*, you were amazing.' Smiling at the little girl, Nikos dropped the remains of the suture on the dressing trolley, stripped off his gloves and left the room without once glancing at Ella.

Feeling like a student nurse in her first week of training, Ella discharged the child, tidied the room and made a decision.

She couldn't do this.

She couldn't concentrate on her work while she was consumed with anxiety about their next confrontation.

So far she'd done less than six hours of her shift and already she was a basket case. His words were going round and round in her head and the injustice of it all was building up inside her.

How *dared* he turn this situation into something that was her fault when he was the one who had lied?

What right did he have to be angry with her?

Heart thumping, she went to look for him and found him in his office, talking in clipped, decisive tones to someone who was clearly giving him a battery of excuses for the deplorable staffing levels.

'Take another look at your budget,' Nikos advised in a silky tone, his gaze resting on Ella as she hovered in the doorway. 'Yes, I can prepare you a case if you need me to.' His jaw tightened. 'No, I can't come at four o'clock. At four o'clock I will be working, staffing this department that has murals and toys, but insufficient staff. Call the meeting for nine o'clock—well, if most of them have already left by then, they're luckier than the rest of us. Perhaps the timing will help reinforce the point I'm trying to make.' He replaced the phone and raised an eyebrow in her direction. 'Is this business or personal? Because if it's personal, I don't have time.'

'Then make time.' Suddenly she almost felt sorry for the hospital's management board. She knew only too well that his kind, approachable side only extended to his young patients. When it came to adults who didn't follow his way of thinking, Nikos was a hard, ruthless adversary. 'I need to talk to you *now*.' With a decisive push of her hand she closed the door firmly behind her and came straight to the point. 'You have no right to be angry with me, because *you* are the one at fault here. It isn't just the fact that you broke up with me or that you're married. You lied to me. You weren't who you said you were.'

'You think I'm faking being a doctor?'

'That isn't what I mean and you know it. Don't play word games with me!' She stabbed her finger towards him, a sudden rush of emotion almost choking her. 'You're a billionaire with loads of houses and yachts and—and—you own super de luxe hotels around the world and—*I had a right to know those things about you.*'

'Why?' Arrogantly male, he held her gaze, displaying not a hint of regret or remorse. 'What difference does it make?'

'It makes a huge difference. How do you think I felt when I found out that you're a billionaire?'

The derisory lift of his brows indicated that the issue wasn't one that interested him. 'Like you'd missed out, I should imagine.'

If she hadn't already slapped him she would have considered doing it now.

'It isn't about the money! I wish you didn't have money because then that would be once less thing you lied about! I felt betrayed, Nikos! That's how I felt.' Ella felt a rush of despair that he didn't seem to understand why she might have been upset. 'You lied about who you were and you lied about your wife! Pictures of your wedding were plastered all over the magazine I picked up in the doctor's surgery. How *could* you? How *could* you have sex with me when you're married? Don't you have a conscience?' Immediately after she'd asked the question she regretted it because she could feel her voice start to wobble. 'What was I, Nikos?

An easy lay while you were in London?' Oh God, that was another question she shouldn't have asked.

She was nothing to him, that's what she was.

His eyes grew suddenly cold. 'You are the mother of my child. Don't cheapen yourself!'

'You're the one who did that,' Ella said hoarsely, 'by sleeping with me when you were married to another woman. You cheapened me, Nikos, and you cheapened our relationship. If you're so rich, why didn't you just use some of that money to fly her over from Greece to satisfy your red-hot sex drive?' She was trembling with hot, stinging emotion but he simply watched her in silence, his cool control a stark contrast to her fiery outburst.

'You are jealous.'

'To be jealous I'd have to care about you and I don't care about you, Nikos. I stopped caring when you didn't even have the guts to end it face to face.' Her voice cracked and she stopped talking, afraid to say more. But already it was too late. He was rising to his feet. Walking across to her with the same sense of purpose that characterised everything he did.

'For a woman who claims not to care, you are *extremely* upset.'

Tension sizzled between them and she took a step backwards, rejecting the immediate response of her body. 'Leave me alone, Nikos. We'll work together for now because we have to, but we don't have to talk about anything personal. You're angry with me and frankly I'm angry with you, too.'

Most of all she was angry that she still cared.

She didn't want to feel what she was feeling.

'When you're angry, your eyes go darker.' His eyes

shielded by impossibly thick lashes, he locked his fingers with hers, trapping her hands in his. 'The same thing happens when you are really, really aroused. Yes, we're both angry. We are both passionate people. Passionate people experience strong emotions.' His hands moved over hers and Ella gritted her teeth because those strong, knowing fingers were as skilful at arousing a woman as they were at healing a patient. Excitement slammed through her body, replacing anger with a much more dangerous emotion.

The air around them seemed stiflingly hot and suddenly she couldn't think or breathe.

Where had the anger gone? She needed it. She needed it back.

'Why did you come here, Nikos?'

His response to that was to lower his head and capture her mouth, using his intimate knowledge of her to drive her straight from earth to paradise without a pause. He kissed her with merciless skill and erotic expertise, his possessive hands capturing her face and holding her while the sensual lick of his tongue robbed her brain of thought and her legs of strength.

Despite her best intentions, her arms wound themselves round his neck, her fingers dug into his sleek, dark hair and Ella moaned in desperation as she felt his weight press her hard against the wall. Her body melted into the demands of his—soft against hard, compliant against aggressive.

'*Theos mou*, you turn me on,' he breathed against her mouth, and Ella felt her senses spin, and every one of her brain cells fuse.

They were so lost in each other that neither of them heard the door open.

'Dr Mariakos?' Rose didn't get any further than his name before muttering an embarrassed apology and slinking out of the room, but her interruption was enough to break the fierce passion that had held them in its grip.

'Nikos…' Groaning his name, Ella pushed against the hard muscle of his chest, but he was apparently in no hurry to release her. His hands rested on the curve of her bottom, his mouth lingering on her neck. 'Nikos—for goodness' sake. Stop.'

Slowly he lifted his head, terminating the embrace in his own time. 'What's wrong?'

Ella suddenly felt sick because he was so sure of himself and she was so confused about everything and he'd just made things a thousand times worse.

'Damn you, Nikos.' Her voice was hoarse. 'How *dare* you do that? I work here. I have a reputation.'

'Kissing the father of your baby has no impact on your ability to heal the sick.' Unapologetic, Nikos straightened and there was a flicker of satisfaction in his eyes as they lingered briefly on the tell-tale jut of her breasts under the blue scrub suit. 'Your breasts are fantastic.'

'You know what?' Boiling with rage, every part of her body throbbing, Ella glared at him. 'If that uncontrollable sex drive of yours is bothering you, then next time phone your wife and make some arrangement with her. I'm not interested.'

He stepped away from her, his expression cold.

'Next time you pick up a magazine, take the trouble to read the words that go with the pictures.' His face was oddly pale under his tan. 'Those photographs were taken sixteen years ago, on my wedding day. And they were published a few months ago to commemorate the anniversary of an accident. My wife is dead, Ella. She was killed fifteen years ago, along with my baby daughter.'

What had possessed her to come for a drink when she didn't feel in the least bit sociable?

Tense, jumpy and unbelievably upset, Ella sat on the harbour wall outside the pub, nursing a glass of orange juice as she stared at the boats. The night was still warm, and behind her The Lobster Pot was alive with laughter as locals and tourists spilled out of the open doors.

The pub on the water was a favourite meeting spot and the team from the emergency department had observed their usual Friday night tradition and were gathered around their favourite table, overlooking the harbour.

Ella had been persuaded to join them and hadn't been able to come up with a ready excuse, even though she'd known she was going to be lousy company.

One drink, she promised herself, *and then she'd leave*.

She'd changed back into the same shorts and shirt that she'd cycled to work in and the cool stones of the wall scraped against the back of her legs. But she had no inclination to join the rest of them at the table.

She didn't feel capable of making conversation or talking about her day.

Her head was still in a spin.

His wife was dead?

She'd had no idea.

Of course she was only human so she'd sneaked off to the computer and typed her question into a search engine—something she would have done months earlier had she not been so sure that she already had the answers.

Remembering what she'd discovered, Ella gave a sigh.

No wonder the man locked himself away emotionally.

He'd lost a wife and a child.

Her thoughts a confused and tangled mess, she watched the tourists wandering along the harbour, eating fish and chips from the paper. Below her, on one of the little boats, a couple with young children were eating hot dogs and laughing together.

Ella envied their happiness. They made family life look simple. Straightforward.

But it wasn't that easy, was it?

Looking at the father, she wondered what secrets he was hiding behind his benevolent smile.

How long before revelations tore this perfect family unit down the middle?

Her fingers tightened around her glass and she thought of Nikos, and of how angry he was with her.

They'd been together for six months and yet he'd never mentioned his wife and child.

She'd thought they were close.

With a bitter laugh, she took a sip of her drink. Physically, they'd been close. But not emotionally. He hadn't confided in her.

And she hadn't confided in him either, had she?

Ella rubbed her aching forehead with her fingers, wondering why life always had to be so complicated.

At least she wouldn't see him again until tomorrow. She had time to think about what to do for the best. The truth was she didn't want to let Ruth down and she didn't want to leave her job. But today had proved that she wasn't capable of working with him.

'Unless you want lots of questions, you should smile.' Helen joined her, a heaped bowl of crisps in her hand.

'You look as though you're contemplating jumping head first into the water. Judging from your expression, I'm guessing the reunion wasn't what you were hoping.'

Her stomach churning, Ella refused the crisps, aware that she was the object of speculation. 'You've heard that he's here, then. Is everyone gossiping? Do they all know?'

'That you're involved with the gorgeous Greek? Of course. He was kissing you as though it was your last moments on earth. I have to say that if a man ever kissed me like that it probably would be. I'd die of ecstasy. The sparks have been crackling between the two of you all afternoon. It's like pouring water onto chip fat.'

Ella stared at her friend. 'What are they saying?'

'Well—you know what the department is like.' Helen was obviously searching for the most tactful response. 'Everyone is desperate for light relief. It probably took less than four seconds for everyone to find out that the two of you are involved. From then on they were drawing straws as to who could go and help out in Paeds Emergency so that they could spy on the situation.'

'Great.' Every muscle in her body was tense, her head ached with endless thinking and her senses still hummed from a day spent within touching distance of Nikos.

Helen was steadily munching her way through the crisps. 'I told them you moved down here first because Nikos couldn't get away from London and that you didn't mention it because you didn't want people feeling awkward.'

'Thanks. That was kind of you.' Ella picked a piece of ice out of her glass. 'I'm sorry I yelled at you earlier. You've been so good to me. I didn't mean to be a grouch. I overreacted. I know you were only trying to help.'

'*I'm* the one who's sorry. Sorry for what I did.'

'I didn't tell you the whole story, so in a way it was my fault.'

'Well, I'm still sorry.' Helen pulled a face. '*Obviously* when I wrote that letter I didn't think for a moment that he'd actually take a job here. Hospital management must have thought it was their lucky day, finding a doctor of his calibre.'

'I'm sure they did.' Ella thought about his clinical skills—about the way he was with every child he treated. 'And maybe you did me a favour. At least now I don't have to spend another night agonising about whether to tell him or not.'

'So how did he take the news that he's going to be a dad?'

Ella tightened her grip on the glass. 'Well, it was hardly a loving reunion, if that's what you're asking.' And she was still shocked by how angry he was.

She'd been naïve, she realised, to think he might have apologised.

He wasn't the sort of man who ever felt the need to apologise because he never entertained the possibility that he could be wrong about anything.

Helen put the bowl of crisps carefully down on the wall. 'Ella, he came after you. What's the situation with his wife? Did you ask him? Are they heading for divorce or something?'

Ella glanced at her colleagues, all laughing at something Rose had said. 'His wife is dead. She died in a car accident fifteen years ago along with his daughter.'

And she was still reeling from the discovery.

He'd lost his family.

No wonder he was cold and emotionally detached. It was probably the only way he could survive.

'Oh, my God, that's terrible.' Helen lifted her hand to

her mouth. 'How can he work in the emergency department? Doesn't it remind him?'

'I've no idea. I don't know the details. He isn't exactly given to talking about his feelings.' And that hurt more than she could have imagined possible.

A relationship without trust was just sex, she thought numbly.

'So why did that magazine publish wedding photographs?'

'It was the anniversary of the accident, or something. I think he gave money and opened a children's hospital in Athens.' She gave a twisted smile. 'Unfortunately I didn't bother reading the words that went with the photos, so I missed the bit that mentioned the accident.' *And she'd hurt him.*

'That's really sad,' Helen said quietly. 'But it was obviously a long time ago. He must be over it now, Ella.'

'Is he?' Ella thought about what she knew of him. 'I don't think so. And do you ever really get over something like that? I'm not sure you do. You live with it. You cope, because you have to. It explains a lot about the way he is—the fact that he won't commit to anyone. I've looked him up on the internet.' Ella kept her voice light. 'He has a reputation for moving around. He doesn't stay in the same place for long, or with the same woman.'

Helen touched her arm in a gesture of female solidarity. 'Ella, he came to find you. That has to mean something.'

'It means a great deal of inconvenience.' Ella toyed with her glass. 'One of us is going to have to leave.'

'That's a bit extreme, isn't it? You work really well together. You're a fantastic team.'

'We *were* a fantastic team.' Ella corrected her softly. 'We *were* a lot of things. But the only thing we are now is over. I honestly don't think I can work alongside him. I feel dreadful about his wife and daughter, of course I do. But he kept so much from me, Helen. He kept a whole life from me. I can't be with a man like that. At the moment I can't even bear to talk to him.'

'Well, if that's really the way you feel then things are about to get a little awkward,' Helen muttered, her eyes fixed on a point further round the harbour wall. 'That deliciously sexy man of yours has just parked his equally sexy car on the street and is striding towards us as we speak. He isn't exactly the hesitant sort, is he? Oh, my—I'd forgotten just how breathtaking he is to look at. If I had him in my bed I'd keep the lights on and my eyes open. I'm sorry, Ella, but it's really hard to feel sorry for you. Rich, clever and a body to die for. The gods tripped when they made him and spilt all their gifts in one place.'

Ella turned, saw Nikos, and the glass of juice slipped from her hand and shattered. Mortified and exasperated with herself, she stooped to retrieve the pieces only to find herself hauled to her feet by strong, determined hands.

'*Theos mou*, do you want to cut yourself to pieces?' Incredulity and concern lighting his dark eyes, Nikos raised a hand and attracted the attention of one of the bar staff. A young girl with a cheerful smile and a blonde ponytail immediately hurried over to deal with the glass while Helen tactfully melted away and joined the group gathered around the large wooden table.

Wondering what Nikos was doing there, Ella looked at him warily. 'If you're about to lose your temper again, I'd rather you didn't do it in public.'

His dark, speculative gaze rested on hers. 'You don't think I have reason to be angry?'

'Maybe you do. I don't know. This whole situation is—' She broke off, uncomfortably aware that she'd been horribly tactless earlier. Whatever their differences, she couldn't bear the fact that she'd hurt someone. 'I didn't know about your wife and child. I'm sorry. I—I'm sorry if I upset you.'

Before Nikos could respond, Billy, the paramedic, strolled across to them.

Ella sighed. *It was going to be impossible to have a conversation here.* They had no more privacy than they'd had at work.

'Good to see you here, boss.' Billy grinned at Nikos and slung his arm around Ella's shoulders in a friendly gesture. 'Is she too drunk to hold a glass? Can't take her anywhere. One drink and she's anybody's. What were you drinking, beautiful?'

'She isn't anybody's—she's mine,' Nikos said in a cool tone, 'and she'll drink what I buy her.'

Billy took one look at his face and removed his arm from Ella's shoulders with exaggerated care.

'Obviously a man of taste. Given that you've got bigger shoulders than me and you're about a foot taller, I'm going to concede defeat.' With a good-natured grin, he wandered off to join the group gathered round the table, leaving Ella with burning cheeks.

'Thanks for embarrassing me.'

Nikos glanced at her, unrepentant. 'He had his arm round you.'

'He was being friendly.'

'You're too naïve to know the difference between

friendly and flirting.' His tone was pleasant but his eyes glinted midnight black. 'That was flirting.'

'So what if it was? He was just having fun. What's wrong with that?'

'Nothing.' Nikos rested a lean hip against the wall, his voice deceptively mild. 'Providing he has no wish to fulfil his full life expectancy.'

Ella gave a strangled laugh. 'You're such a contradiction. You stand there all sophisticated in your, oh, so expensive suit and yet underneath you're so primitive you should be wearing a loincloth and wrestling lions with your bare hands.'

Nikos shrugged. 'I know how to protect what's mine.'

Shocked by the slow, dangerous curl of awareness in her stomach, Ella breathed deeply. 'I'm not yours.'

'You're carrying my child.'

'And that means that no other man can speak to me?'

'He can look,' Nikos drawled softly, 'but he can't touch.'

Ella shook her head in disbelief. 'As I said—primitive. You're a doctor. You're supposed to heal the sick.'

'I would have healed him—' his smile was dangerous '—after I'd beaten him up for being too familiar with you.'

The knowledge that he wasn't married changed everything, even though she didn't want it to. 'You're behaving like a caveman.'

'He is interested in you. It's only fair to let him know that he doesn't stand a chance in hell. I saved him from disappointment.'

'How do you know he doesn't stand a chance?' Ella felt her heart race in a rhythm all of its own. 'It's my decision who I see. I'm not your property, Nikos. Our relationship is over.' *He'd lied to her*, she reminded herself desperately. And he was clearly incapable of emotional commitment.

Maybe he wasn't married, but as a partner he was bad news.

His dark eyes locked on hers. *Those clever, all-seeing doctor's eyes.* 'You're carrying my child.'

The sexual chemistry between them was so powerful that she couldn't breathe. 'That's a separate issue.'

'*Not* to a Greek male.'

'It's a little late to be possessive, Nikos.' She shook her head. 'What are you doing here, anyway? Why did you come here tonight?'

'To say the things I should have said this afternoon and didn't. I'll get you another drink. Then we can talk.'

'In public?'

He gave a faint smile. 'I hoped it might force us both to be calm and rational.'

Aware of the curious stares of the rest of the group, Ella fixed a smile on her face. She watched as he strolled over and greeted everyone, his comments delivered with a light, masterly touch that guaranteed his immediate acceptance into this group of strangers.

There was warmth and a large dollop of deference in the attitude of the rest of the team and Ella gritted her teeth because his charisma and unmistakable leadership qualities had had a similar effect on her at one time. Progress and equality had apparently done nothing to diminish the attractions of a powerful man, she thought wryly, and Nikos Mariakos wore responsibility as comfortably as he wore the sleek designer suit that skimmed his broad shoulders.

He addressed a few words to the group, made them laugh with an astute observation and then secured his place as one of them by inviting them to order at his expense.

It was a mark of respect and an acknowledgement of his

reputation and seniority that someone offered him a chair, but he declined, spoke to someone behind the bar and then settled his lean hips against the harbour wall, next to Ella.

Her hand was on the wall and he placed his over it, long strong fingers covering hers in a gesture that said 'mine' as clearly as if he'd sprayed the word in red on the bricks.

A few months ago Ella would have found such a macho display amusing. She also would have found it hopelessly flattering, although she would never in a million years have admitted it to anyone. Now, when she turned her head, her eyes were mocking. 'Unreconstructed Greek,' she murmured, and he gave a wry smile, his fingers locking with hers.

'Perhaps. In some things at least. Have you eaten?'

'You put me off my food.'

His laugh was soft. 'Your heart may be broken, but I see your spirit is intact.' He glanced briefly towards the others but they'd already lost interest and were now involved in a heated debate about the use of the air ambulance.

Ella was painfully aware of the press of his hard thigh against hers, the gentle caress of his fingers on hers. For her own protection, she wanted to snatch her hand away but she didn't want to draw the attention of the group.

'This is a low trick because I can't slap you in public. What is it that you want, Nikos?'

'You.' His gaze was focused on her mouth. 'I want you, *agape mou*. Back in my bed, where you belong.'

His words robbed her of breath. 'Why?' It was hard to keep it light. 'None of your relationships have lasted more than six months. I'm already past my sell-by date.'

His hand tightened on hers. 'I think we have already proved that it is dangerous to jump to conclusions.'

The touch of his hand was enough to make her insides

clench. 'You walked out on me. There's no way I'd be foolish enough to get involved with you again, Nikos.'

'We are involved. The child you are carrying links us together.'

It was dark now, and the tiny fairy-lights illuminating the pub made the atmosphere magical. Behind them the masts of the boat clinked in the breeze and the air was filled with everything that was summer—garlic from the pub, the salt from the sea and the cool breath of wind.

'This isn't going to work, Nikos.' Ella spoke softly, acutely aware of the curious looks they were receiving from other members of the department. 'Why did you come here?'

'If you don't know why I came,' he replied, 'then you don't know me at all.'

'You're right, I don't know you. I spent six months with you and then discovered that you weren't who I thought you were. You didn't mention the money.' She swallowed, not wanting to deliberately hurt someone but aware of the enormity of what they were dealing with. 'You didn't mention that you'd lost your wife.'

He was still. 'You want to have this conversation here?'

'I don't want to have the conversation at all. We have nothing to talk about. We had an affair. Now it's over. It happens. You can see your child, Nikos, if that's what's worrying you.' She rubbed her hands up her arms, chilled even though the night was warm. 'We'll work something out.'

'*Theos mou*, you stand there offering me visitation rights? You think that's what I want?' His voice was fierce and Ella froze, horrified at the thought that people might hear.

'Keep your voice down. I don't know what you want. I thought you wanted to see your child. But if you don't—

that's fine, too. I suppose your latest girlfriend would take a pretty dim view of having a relationship with a guy who has a baby in tow.'

Nikos made an impatient sound. 'I do not have a girl-friend. Since we parted I have been working in Athens at the children's hospital. And that is enough talking about the past. We need to talk about the future.'

Keeping the lock and chain firmly on her dreams, Ella blinked back tears. 'We don't have a future, Nikos.'

'Be careful…' he gave a dangerous smile, his fingers trapping hers '…or I might just choose to prove you wrong in public.'

They stood for a moment, a host of things unsaid, and then Rose strolled across to them.

'Your car is attracting quite a crowd, Nikos.' She cast an amused glance towards the group of teenagers who were loitering on the street, gazing in awe at the sleek lines of Nikos's high-performance sports car. 'Dare I ask how the meeting with the hospital management board went? I suppose they turned you down?'

Dragging his hot, burning gaze from Ella's face, Nikos turned his attention to Rose, visibly struggling to concentrate. 'From next Monday the budget will cover three extra nurses for the summer months, one of them paediatric trained.'

Rose gave a gasp of shocked delight. 'You're joking.'

'There is no humourous side to health service staffing,' Nikos drawled, and Rose stood on tiptoe and hugged him impulsively.

'You're a genius. Oh, sorry.' Embarrassed, she sat down and cast Ella an apologetic look. 'It's just that we've been so stretched and our numbers seem to go up every summer. What did you say to them?'

'I appealed to their sense of reason,' Nikos said silkily, and Ella rolled her eyes.

'You bullied them.'

'I was forcefully persuasive,' Nikos countered, and Rose laughed.

'I love that. Forcefully persuasive. Remind me to adopt that approach next Saturday night when the department is full of drunks. Forcefully persuasive.' Grinning with delight, she wandered back to the table to pass on the happy news to the rest of the team.

'So now you're a hero.' Her stomach churning, Ella abandoned all hope of relaxing. 'Well—given that you've secured extra staff, no one will miss me if I leave. I'm going to hand in my resignation tomorrow.'

'There is no reason for you to resign.'

'I cannot work alongside my ex-lover.' Suddenly Ella felt exhausted.

Pregnancy or stress?

Below her in the harbour the family on the boat were putting the children to bed and Ella swallowed down the lump in her throat as she noticed the tiny stuffed bear in one of the windows.

They were a family.

Whatever that meant.

Her mind flew back to the moment that she'd discovered that she was pregnant. She'd been too devastated by what she'd discovered about Nikos to feel excited about her own news.

And even knowing that part of it had been a misunderstanding, there was no getting away from the fact that he had lied about the money. And he hadn't trusted her enough to share the details of his past.

Secrets.

'You're tired.' Nikos straightened, slid a possessive arm around her shoulders and uttered a smooth apology to the rest of the group. 'We've been apart for rather too long. If you'll excuse us…'

Ella resisted the temptation to brush him off simply because she didn't want the gossip.

As they walked along the street, the crowd of teenage boys hovering around Nikos's car parted with silent deference.

'Great car, man,' one of them breathed enviously, and Nikos made a masculine comment about cylinders or something equally unfathomable, and Ella took advantage of the brief distraction to make her escape.

'I'll leave you to it. My super-charged, no-cylinder pushbike is chained to the railings back there. I'll give you a head start so that I don't dent that massive ego of yours by overtaking you.' She turned to walk away but he closed his fingers around her wrist, anchoring her to his side.

'You are not cycling home in the dark.'

'Why not?'

'Don't goad me, Ella,' he growled. 'I will give you a lift. And then I'll arrange to have your bike collected and delivered to the hospital.'

'How?' Ella kicked against his tendency to take control in every situation. 'Don't tell me—you have a team of staff just waiting to do your bidding.'

'Just get in the car.'

She wanted to argue, but the truth was she was so exhausted that she wasn't sure she would be able to pedal as far as the boat.

With the luck she'd had so far today, she'd end up in the canal.

This time, she thought, *he can take charge*. Just this time.

'This isn't a car, it's a spaceship.' And it was gorgeous, she thought weakly. Sleek, elegant lines. Expensive. Sophisticated. *Out of her league*.

'Ella,' he said tightly, 'just get in.'

Too tired to argue, Ella sank into the luxurious leather seat and he settled his lean, athletic frame in the seat next to her, pressed a button and the engine started with a throaty growl.

'I don't know why you're so angry with me,' she muttered. 'You were the one who walked out on me.'

'We've talked about this enough for one night.'

'Is this a billionaire car? It's only got two seats—you were ripped off.' Her tone flippant, Ella suppressed a yawn and let her head rest back against the seat. 'So where are you staying? Do you realise that when we were together you never let me see your home? I expect you were living in some fancy house, weren't you? Why didn't you want me to know?'

'Because money changes everything.'

'I wouldn't know.' Ella closed her eyes. 'I've never had any. Where are you living now? Don't tell me. You own a luxury penthouse with a sea view?'

'No, *agape mou*.' Controlling the car with smooth precision, Nikos executed a perfect U-turn and headed away from the harbour. 'I'm staying with the mother of my child. So where are we living at the moment?'

CHAPTER THREE

A CANAL boat?

She was living alone on a canal boat?

A torch in his teeth and a sleeping woman in his arms, Nikos cursed mentally, wondering how people who were not blessed with long legs managed to stretch the distance between the bank and the deck.

The hazards were too numerous to be counted.

The towpath that led from the boat to the road was unlit and overgrown, and the thought of who might be lurking in the shadows watching a woman on her own on a boat brought him out in goose-bumps.

Why had she chosen to live in a place like this?

What was she trying to prove?

Following the directions she'd drowsily given him before she'd fallen asleep, he'd parked in a deserted picnic spot next to the towpath and then walked the remaining distance to the boat, his tension mounting with every stride.

It was a security nightmare, and she was living alone.

Tomorrow he'd move her out of here, he vowed swiftly.

The scent of her blonde hair teased his senses and Nikos gritted his teeth as he unlocked the door and ducked down into the boat with her still in his arms.

Despite his efforts he still smacked his head hard on the top of the door and grunted in pain as he flashed the torch around the interior of the boat.

He needed lights. Did a boat like this one have lights?

Aware that he was less than three centimetres away from being knocked unconscious on the roof, Nikos placed her gently on the sofa.

The thought of her living somewhere so isolated brought him out in a cold sweat and he made a mental note never to let her spend five minutes on her own here again. And if that meant moving into this floating equivalent of a suitcase, then so be it.

With a grim sense of purpose he found a light and switched it on, his impression of the place not improving as an army of insects from the river swarmed towards the glow. Closing the doors, he strode down the length of the boat, cast an appalled glance at the small double bed wedged in between two cupboards and gazed in disbelief at the small bath.

How was a guy supposed to wash in that?'

Deciding that the bed should just be able to accommodate his six-foot-three frame if he slept diagonally, Nikos returned to the living area, carefully scooped Ella into his arms and transferred her onto the more comfortable mattress.

Still she didn't wake and he shrugged off his jacket and hooked it carelessly over the corner of a convenient door, his eyes scanning her pale face and the dark shadows under her eyes, the result, he presumed, of either the pregnancy or stress or both.

Recalling her stricken expression as dressings and instruments had slipped from her shaking fingers, Nikos experienced an uncomfortable surge of guilt as he acknowledged the role he'd played in raising her stress levels.

So much for being calm and rational.

All his intentions about not losing his temper had flown out of the window when he'd seen her. He was still angry, but now the anger was permeated with a very different emotion, and it was that emotion that made him bend down and gently ease off her shoes and cover her sleeping form with a blanket.

She was trying to shut him out, but she wasn't going to succeed.

As far as he was concerned, this situation could only have one outcome.

'Ella?' He spoke her name roughly but still she didn't stir, her lashes forming perfect crescents on her pale cheeks, her pink lips slightly parted as she slept.

Discovering that his skills at undressing a woman didn't extend to the sleeping variety, it took Nikos endless minutes and much personal frustration to part her lush body from her clothes. Deciding that removing her underwear wouldn't earn him any thanks, he slid the covers over her.

Then he emptied the pockets of his jacket, undressed swiftly and slid into the bed next to her, gently shifting her position so that there was room for both of them.

In sleep she nestled against him and he tensed as he felt the instant, fierce response of his body.

This was the reason he'd ended their relationship.

His feelings for her had been growing and he'd promised himself that that was never going to happen to him again.

But that was before he'd discovered that she was having his baby.

That changed everything.

* * *

Ella woke to the sound of ducks and the glare of sunlight. For a moment she just lay there, smiling sleepily to herself, the sounds of nature acting like a sedative.

Gradually her brain returned to consciousness and she was dimly aware that her hand felt strange. Turning her head slightly, she realised that she was lying against a strong male shoulder and that Nikos was sprawled next to her, the tangle of bedcovers revealing tantalising glimpses of his gloriously naked body.

'Nikos?! What are you doing in my bed?' Aghast, she sat up instantly, clutching the sheet against her. 'Get out of here!'

'Go back to sleep.'

His eyes remained closed and she was temporarily distracted by his thick, dark eyelashes. Even half-asleep he was extravagantly handsome, his hard jaw darkened by stubble, his mouth a firm, sensual line in a face that might have been designed by the gods to tempt a woman to ditch common sense and morals and live for the moment.

Oh, God, no wonder she'd abandoned years of caution.

A dangerous weakness spread through her limbs and she desperately tried to summon up the anger that she'd felt for the last four months.

Lies, she reminded herself. *Lies, lies and more lies.*

All right, so technically he wasn't married. But there was still the fact that he hadn't told her the truth about himself, not to mention his reputation for never becoming involved with women.

'Get out of my bed, Nikos.' She spoke through gritted teeth and he gave a slow, confident smile.

'Why? Don't you trust yourself to be this close to me? I thought we were over. I thought you didn't feel anything for me any more, *agape mou*.'

'I was wrong about that.' Ella tugged at the sheet, covering herself. 'I do feel something. I feel like thumping you. Hard.'

'You already did that.' His eyes opened. 'If you're planning to do it again, don't use your left hand. You might do me serious injury.'

Puzzled, not understanding his comment, she glanced down at her left hand and stopped breathing. A ring sparkled and gleamed in the early morning sunlight—a beautiful diamond, so large that Ella just stared at it in disbelief.

'What,' she muttered faintly, 'is that?'

No wonder her hand had felt strange. She was carrying the equivalent of half her body weight on her ring finger.

'It's a ring.' He raised himself on his elbows, the muscles in his powerful shoulders flexing as he supported his weight. 'My ring. You will wear it.'

'Why would I want to do that? You may not be married, Nikos, but I'm still not interested.'

'You're having my baby. You'll wear the ring.' Nikos leaned back against the pillows, sickeningly handsome and incredibly sure of himself. 'It will keep other men at a distance while I make the necessary arrangements for our wedding.' He spoke in such a cool, factual tone that she mentally reran his words through her head a second time, sure that she must have misunderstood him.

Wedding? 'Did you say *wedding*? You have to be kidding. *You're asking me to marry you?*'

'Why else would I have put a rare diamond on your finger?'

'I've no idea. To be flashy, I suppose. Because your billionaire secret is out of the bag? And because it's easier to buy a gift than have a conversation?' Genuinely shocked, Ella scooted away from him, her mouth so dry she could hardly speak. 'Nikos, how can you possibly propose to me after everything that has happened?'

'Why not?'

He was proposing to her?

How many times had she lain there at night, imagining this exact scenario?

How many times during their blissful six months had she dreamt about him asking her to marry him?

More times than she could count.

And then that dream had been blown away by the discovery that he had a wife. Only, she knew now that he didn't.

She could just say yes, she thought weakly, and for a moment temptation was there, dangled in front of her in the form of this undeniably gorgeous man whom she adored. She could ignore everything that had happened, say yes and her dream would become reality.

Except that it wouldn't, would it?

Her dream had never been about wearing a rock on her finger or choosing a frothy wedding dress. Her dream hadn't been about bridesmaids, honeymoons or even exchanging vows.

Her dream had been about pledging to share her life with someone she loved and trusted, who loved and trusted her in return.

Where was the love and trust in their relationship?

How could she say yes to a man who had lied to her? *Who kept so much of himself locked away?*

'No.' The word emerged as a cracked whisper, as if her body knew that she didn't really want to say that word.

His eyes narrowed with incomprehension. 'No, what?'

'No, I can't marry you. There is no way I'd *ever* marry you, Nikos. I can't honestly believe that you'd think I would.'

He stilled, his shock at her refusal as great as hers had been at his unexpected proposal. 'You are having my child.'

And that was why he was here, of course. That was why she was currently wearing an enormous diamond on her finger.

'You left me, Nikos.' Saying the words was a painful reality check. 'You didn't want to be with me.'

'When I left you, you weren't having my baby.'

Ella turned her head, struggling for control. 'If you didn't want me before I was pregnant, why would you want me now that I am?'

'The answer to that is self-evident.'

She swallowed back the hurt. 'A baby isn't a reason to get married. A child is not a good enough reason to get married, Nikos! Marriage is about love and trust and feelings—' She broke off, feeling a flash of despair because here he was proposing and she was turning him down. 'Two people shouldn't marry just because they've made a baby. It isn't enough.'

'What are you saying?' He raised an eyebrow, a sardonic smile touching his sexy mouth. 'The diamond isn't big enough?'

She gritted her teeth. 'I'm saying that a ring can't fix what's wrong between us. All this ring does is remind me that you're a billionaire and that you kept that fact from me.' She began to slide out of the bed but he hauled her back down, rolled her onto her back and covered her body with his.

'We are talking. Don't walk away.'

'Let me go, Nikos!' She tried to wriggle away from

him but the slide of her thigh against his sent a tremor of sexual awareness through her body. She went still. 'This is crazy! You're a billionaire and I made you cheese on toast.'

Amusement shimmered in his dark gaze. 'I love your cheese on toast.'

'We slept in my single bed—'

'Which was extremely cosy,' he murmured, bringing his mouth close to hers.

'I don't even know you!'

For a highly charged moment he just looked at her and she was desperately conscious of his weight pressing her into the mattress. 'You don't know me?' He shifted deliberately, and she gave a soft gasp as she felt his body come into intimate contact with hers. 'Tell me something, *pethi mou*—just how much more of me do you want to know?'

'Nikos—'

'I love the way you say my name.' His smile was lazily possessive and he lowered his mouth to hers with the confidence of a man who had never known rejection.

His kiss made her tremble in the way that it always had and probably always would. And all the time his mouth feasted on hers, his fingers skimmed her body until Ella's skin was so sensitised that she felt as though she was on fire.

He shifted slightly in order to allow himself better access and her body thrilled with excitement at his skilled touch.

It was the possessive stroke of his hand over her softly rounded abdomen that brought her to her senses.

'No.' For him, this was all about the baby. 'No, Nikos. I'm not going to let you do this to me again.' Ignoring the wild crazy pulse of sexual attraction that drew them together, she pushed him away and slid out of the bed before the maddening ache in her body drove all resistance from her. 'We get into bed and we don't think about anything else! We don't think about what's right or sensible. We don't have a proper relationship! We're not doing this again.' She licked her lips—tried to shut her reaction down. 'And stop looking at me like that!'

His hooded gaze was fixed on her semi-naked body in pure masculine appraisal and she gave a murmur of exasperation that was directed entirely at herself, before grabbing a large T-shirt from the bag that she still hadn't unpacked. She dragged it over her head with such haste that it took her a moment of struggling to find the armholes. Then she scooped her hair free and walked down the narrow corridor that led to the kitchen area and the living room, her body screaming a protest.

Every part of her was aroused, warm and ready.

She wanted him. *Every single part of her wanted him.*

Her hand shook as she filled the kettle, reminding herself that just because you could, it didn't mean you should. *If she was ever interested in a man again it was going to be a calm, sensible Englishman*, she promised herself as she turned on the gas and put the kettle on to boil. *Not a volatile Greek with superior seduction skills.*

For twenty-four years she'd been careful around men. She'd been cautious and wary. Then she'd met Nikos and all that caution had been burnt up in a rush of explosive sexual chemistry.

What was it about the man that made it so hard to do the sensible thing?

Her eyes slid to the diamond on her finger. *The diamond she was still wearing.*

It was stunning, the beautifully cut stone appealing to the woman in her.

It would have been so easy to say yes. A huge part of her wanted to say yes. Yes to marriage, yes to sex, yes to a life with this man.

But how could she say yes when not only had he kept secrets from her but he didn't seem to think there was anything wrong in that?

To gain herself thinking time, she made two cups of coffee and took hers out on the tiny deck at the prow of the boat, instantly calmed by the early morning peace of the canal. The sun played on the surface of the water, casting shadows and light. Nettles and reeds stood guard along the river bank and rhododendrons crowded over the water, as if admiring their own reflections. A swan glided past, watchful of her three cygnets, and Ella felt a pang of kinship for this mother, protecting her young.

Suddenly feeling a huge burden of responsibility, Ella put her hand on the curve of her abdomen, still intrigued by her new shape.

'You need to move off this boat.' Ducking his glossy dark head to avoid the low door, Nikos joined her on the polished wooden deck. He'd pulled on his trousers but nothing else. Curling dark hairs shadowed the muscular contours of his bare chest and his bronzed shoulders gleamed in the morning sunlight. 'It isn't safe.'

Feeling the immediate stirring of her body, Ella sat down as far away from him as possible. 'I like it. It's beautiful here.'

'It's a totally unsuitable place for a woman to live alone.' His tone smooth, he cast her a glance that sent her insides spinning in a whirlpool of highly charged sexual awareness. 'Especially a pregnant woman.'

He'd zipped up his trousers with a casual hand and they rode slightly low on his hips, exposing an unfair amount of bronzed, muscular abdomen.

Why was it, she wondered, *that just a glimpse of those taut abdominals was enough for her to be able to picture him naked?*

Her mouth as dry as a ditch in summer, Ella instinctively pulled her T-shirt lower over her thighs, wishing she'd stopped long enough to find her jeans. 'Who is going to bother me here? There's no one around.'

'Precisely.' Those dark eyes with those long, long lashes shifted to the silent, overgrown towpath. 'It's deserted.'

'I wanted space.'

'Well, you've certainly got that.' His tone ironic, he looked around him with a faint smile. 'It *is* beautiful,' he conceded grimly, 'but there must be safer ways of achieving country living.'

'Not on my budget.' She instantly regretted the words. 'And I don't want your money, Nikos,' she blurted out quickly, 'just in case you think I was dropping a hint.'

He studied her for a long moment. 'Where we live is my responsibility. There is no need to be defensive.'

'I'm not living with you, Nikos.'

He sat down on the seat opposite. The bows of the boat were as narrow as the rest of the craft. With his superior height, their knees were almost touching. 'All right—let's deal with this. You are trying to push me away,' he said harshly, 'but it isn't going to work. That is my baby you are carrying and my ring you're wearing on your finger.'

Heart pounding, Ella twisted the ring round and round her finger. 'I would have thrown it back at you,' she muttered, 'but I thought it would knock you unconscious. You don't do subtle, do you? The ring tells the whole world that you're filthy rich.'

'No, *agape mou*. The ring tells everyone that you are mine.' His eyes stayed on hers. 'I want there to be no misunderstandings.'

She wondered what lay behind that comment but knew that there was no point in asking. He didn't confide in her, did he? There was so much he hadn't told her about himself. 'I am *not* yours, Nikos.'

'Why do you insist on fighting with me?'

'I don't know.' Her tone was flippant. 'Perhaps because you're unbelievably insensitive?'

'Then we must be experiencing a severe cultural clash. No matter how hard I try I cannot see how proposing marriage to the woman carrying my child could be classed as insensitive.'

'Because marriage isn't about reproduction.'

'It is in Greece,' Nikos said dryly, stretching his long legs out as far as he could in the confined space and placing his coffee on the seat. 'In Greece you marry, you have babies.'

'Exactly.' Ella tucked her own legs under her on the seat. 'Marriage first, babies second. We've done it the wrong way round, but that isn't why I'm not going to marry you. I'm refusing to marry you because I don't really know you. The man I was involved with wasn't a billionaire with a tragedy in his past. It's as if you are someone completely different.'

He nursed his coffee, his gaze disturbingly intense. 'I am the same man you gave yourself to every night for six months.'

'No. You keep everything to yourself, Nikos! I can't marry someone like that.'

'The money makes no difference to our relationship.'

'Then why didn't you tell me about it? Did you think I was some greedy gold-digger?'

'Money has an unpredictable effect on people.' He rose to his feet, his voice harsh. 'You've read stories about people who win the lottery and then their lives fall apart. Money changes people. Believe me, I know.'

'Women chase you for your money?' She looked away to hide what she was feeling. *Of course they did.* A man like him would have been chased by women all his life. And not only because of his wealth. 'Why didn't you tell me? Every night you stayed in my tiny room in the nurses' home. We spent six months wrapped round each other in a single bed. At the time I assumed it was just about convenience, but now I'm guessing it was because you didn't want me to see your home.'

He didn't answer immediately. 'What we shared was beautifully uncomplicated. I liked that.'

'It was dishonest.'

'No.' He turned then, his mouth a grim line in his handsome face. 'On the contrary, what I shared with you is probably the only totally honest relationship I've ever had in my life. It was just the two of us. Man and woman.'

Ella found it was hard to breathe.

She didn't want to remember how close they'd been.

'So why didn't you tell me about your past, Nikos?' She watched the ripple of tension spread across his bare shoulders, all the more visible because he was naked from the waist up.

'Because the past isn't relevant.'

'Of course it is. But you didn't trust me enough to talk to me about it, and that's why I can't marry you. By all means be scarily detached in the resuscitation room—I understand that, I really do. But don't do the same thing in a relationship.' She uncurled her legs and tried to stand up, but his hand curled over her shoulder.

'*Theos mou*, you *will* hear me out.' His tone was civilised and restrained, but his eyes glinted hard. 'You can either sit there and listen or I'll carry you back to that space laughingly called a bedroom and find other ways to make you pay attention. Your choice.'

'Why don't you try it?' She placed her hands flat on the wooden seat. 'With luck you might bang that arrogant head of yours.'

He gave a slow smile, impossibly sure of himself. 'I like the passionate side of you. It's the passionate side of your nature that makes our relationship so exciting.'

Ella bit her lip. 'Were you happily married?'

He drained his coffee and took his time answering. 'What difference does it make?'

'I don't know.' She spread her hands helplessly, wondering how to get through to him. 'I suppose I'm just trying to understand something about you.'

'We were both too young,' he said finally, and she sighed.

'What's that supposed to mean? Crazy in love "too young", or stupid "too young"?'

'I was far too idealistic. I wanted to be a doctor, she thought she was marrying a tycoon who would take over the Mariakos family empire.'

'What does the empire consist of? The headline in the magazine mentioned hotels.'

'Hotels, leisure, tourism…' He shrugged. 'Mariakos Industries has diversified over the decades. It is the secret to staying successful in a turbulent economic climate.'

'And you didn't want to be part of that? You didn't want to be involved?'

'It was impossible to grow up in my family and not be involved. As children we were all involved. We virtually lived at the Mariakos Athens and our summers were spent on our island, off the mainland. By the time I was eighteen I knew how to run a hotel and read a balance sheet.'

'But that wasn't what you wanted?'

'I wanted to be a doctor.'

Ella thought of the future that must have stretched in front of him and what a loss it would have been to medicine if he'd taken that path. 'Why?'

He was unnaturally still. 'I was more interested in medicine than hotels.'

Sensing that there was so much more that he wasn't disclosing, Ella suppressed a sigh of frustration. 'Your parents must be proud of you.'

'Now? Yes, they're proud. But back then…' His laugh lacked humour. 'My father was horrified that I wasn't going to take over the business. They thought it was a whim. A teenage rebellion against the life I'd always known. And maybe it was. I don't know.' He shrugged his shoulders dismissively. 'My wife died. I left Greece. I did my training. I started in paediatrics.'

He hadn't mentioned his daughter and something about the hard lines of his jaw stopped Ella from bringing it up, either.

'And you never had another serious relationship?'

'I had relationships, Ella.' There was an ironic glint in his eyes. 'I'm not claiming to have lived the life of a monk.'

But he'd never allowed himself to be close to another woman.

Ella swallowed, remembering Helen's words. 'So was not telling me about the money some sort of test?'

He frowned. 'No. Not a test.'

'I suppose you didn't need to test me because you had no intention of staying with me.'

He didn't deny it. 'I liked the fact that you knew nothing about me. That we had no baggage.'

'Everyone has baggage. We both had baggage, Nikos.' She gave a weak smile. 'It's just that yours was diamond encrusted and mine was cheap plastic.'

He didn't laugh. 'When you discovered that you were pregnant, didn't it occur to you to contact me?'

'I received the news about my pregnancy on the same day I received your email telling me that our relationship was over.' The memory chilled her. 'What was I supposed to do, Nikos? If a relationship is over, it's over. A baby doesn't change that.'

He inhaled deeply and squared his shoulders. 'That's where we disagree.'

'You concealed this huge, huge part of yourself. You thought it didn't matter that I didn't know. What about next time, Nikos? What about next time something happens in your life that you don't think I need to be part of?'

She just couldn't trust him to tell her the truth.

Her imagination raced forward and suddenly she was tortured by an uncomfortably clear image of what the future could hold for her.

Agonising confessions, shock, hardship, devastation and bone-deep loneliness.

She'd seen it all before and she was never going to put herself in that position.

Yes, she loved him. Yes, there was pain. But nothing like

the pain she and the baby would experience if he let them down a few years down the line.

That realisation gave her the final boost she needed to do the most difficult thing she'd ever done in her life.

Ella dragged the ring off her finger. The stone flirted with the sunlight—twinkled and sparkled, trying to seduce her. She stood up and pushed it into his hand. 'I'm very, very sorry about your wife, but I still can't marry you.'

And she ducked through the door and into the boat before he could stop her, discovering that the hardest thing in the world was walking away from something that you really, really wanted.

CHAPTER FOUR

NEVER, if he lived to be a hundred, would he understand women.

Nikos swung his sleek car into his parking space directly outside the paediatric emergency department.

He'd offered her marriage.

He'd put a diamond the size of New York on her finger.

And she'd given it back.

Theos mou, what was going on in her head?

How many women had longed for him to make exactly that gesture?

Was she trying to impress him?

He sprang from the car like a tiger released from captivity and a passing nurse cast a nervous look at his face as he slammed the door and glared at nothing in particular.

He stood there for a moment, thinking. Applying the same analytical skills he used when diagnosing his patients, he examined the facts. He recalled her body language throughout the encounter, remembering her shaking hands and her pale face.

No, she wasn't trying to impress him.

Her refusal had been genuine.

And yet she still wanted him, he knew that.

So why hadn't she just said yes?

Was it about the money?

Or was it to do with the fact he hadn't told her about his wife?

Realising that he didn't have answers to any of the questions made him realise how little he knew about her.

What, in all honesty, had they shared in the six passionate months they'd spent together? *Sex*, he acknowledged ruefully. They'd lived in a small intimate bubble that had involved their work at the hospital and the two of them. Nothing had intruded.

And that had been the way he'd wanted it.

No emotions complicating their relationship.

Only she was a woman, wasn't she?

And women responded better to emotion than logic. Which meant that he needed to alter his approach.

Locking his car, Nikos strode purposefully towards the entrance of the paediatric emergency department, his naturally competitive nature roused by the obstruction she'd placed in the path of their relationship.

She was carrying his baby.

She *would* marry him, he vowed silently. It was just a matter of understanding why she was saying no. Once he understood that, he would turn her no to a yes.

'I'm really, really sorry to be a nuisance,' the woman apologised, 'but I'm just so worried about him.' Her eyes filled and suddenly she burst into tears. 'Twice I've been back to the GP and he just says it's a virus of some sort, but Harry's been crying and crying with the pain in his tummy and— Oh, I don't know, you probably think I'm a stupid time waster...'

'I don't think that, Carol.' Ella slipped an arm around the woman's shoulders and gave her a hug. 'I think you're a very caring mum. A worried, caring mum. And we'll take a good look at little Harry, I promise. Here— have a tissue.' She reached for the box and offered it to Carol. Then she dropped into a crouch so that she could build a relationship with the little boy seated on his mother's lap.

He didn't seem distressed. In fact, he seemed very quiet. Ella frowned.

Too quiet for a little boy who should have been diving straight into the colourful, tempting box of toys near his feet.

'Hello, Harry. How are you doing?' She was expecting a reaction of some sort, but got nothing.

The child just looked at her.

Back in control, Carol blew her nose. 'Sorry. Gosh, this is so embarrassing. I'm not usually like this, only it's been going on for two days and nights and I haven't had any sleep and I'm just exhausted and so worried because no one is taking me seriously and—'

'You have nothing to apologise for. I'm appalling if I don't get my sleep. And we are taking you seriously, Carol.' Ella pulled a toy car out of a nearby box and placed it on the child's lap. 'Look at this, Harry. It's *so* cool. The doors open and the steering-wheel moves— and if you press this switch the lights come on. Do you want a turn?' But Harry showed no interest. He just sat there listlessly and then the next moment he gave a tiny gasp, screwed up his face and clutched his stomach, whimpering in pain.

'You see?' The mother bit her lip. 'He's been doing this for two days. It lasts a few minutes at the most and then it stops. Our doctor just told me to give him paracetamol, but it honestly doesn't make any difference. Oh, for goodness' sake—why am I here? It's probably nothing.'

But Ella wasn't thinking that. Something about the child worried her.

Nothing she could immediately identify. Just an instinct.

Reminding herself that instinct was important when it came to children, she rose to her feet. 'I'm going to ask our consultant to take a look at him.'

She wasn't even sure if Nikos was in the department. After she'd returned his ring, he'd barely said a word to her and she'd had no idea what he was thinking. He'd driven her back to the harbour and waited without saying a word while she'd collected her bike.

Then he'd sped off in a different direction, presumably to his own home to shower and change.

What had he been thinking?

She didn't even know where he was living, she realised as she hurried out of the cubicle and started searching for him.

Somewhere fit for a billionaire, no doubt. An enormous mansion or a glossy penthouse with a view of the sea.

The sort of place designed to showcase a thoroughbred woman dressed in designer silk, sipping her drink while she awaited the Greek Tycoon's pleasure.

Ella chewed her lip anxiously. *Not* the sort of place for a penniless nurse wearing a dress she'd found in a charity shop. And the Greek Tycoon's pleasure wasn't going to be cheese on toast.

Since the death of his wife he'd avoided commitment, and she couldn't risk being with a man like that, could she?

She'd made the right decision. *For both of them.*

The waiting room was crowded with children, a baby was crying and a toddler was using the chairs as a climbing frame.

Kelly, one of the staff nurses from the main emergency department, was standing at the reception desk, looking stressed.

She glanced up with relief as Ella approached. 'I don't know how you do this,' she muttered. 'I mean, the patients are all too young to tell you what's going on. It's all guesswork. And the noise—'

'Have you seen Nikos?' Ella interrupted her swiftly, and the other nurse shook her head.

'He's up with the general manager, thrashing out some problem or other.'

Ella didn't hesitate. 'I need you to call him, Kelly. Tell him there's a patient he needs to see immediately.'

Kelly laughed nervously. 'You're kidding, right? You want me to interrupt a meeting between the chief executive and the Greek god?'

'Don't call him that.' Uncharacteristically irritable, Ella reached for the phone. 'I'll do it myself.' She dialled the switchboard and was instantly put through to the chief executive's office, where she was told he couldn't be disturbed for the next ten minutes.

Ella glanced at the clock on the wall and thought of Harry, listless and quiet on his mother's lap.

It wasn't natural for a two-year-old boy to be listless and quiet.

What if ten minutes was too long?

'I need to speak to Professor Mariakos now,' she said firmly. 'Not in ten minutes.' Ignoring Kelly's awed look, she waited in suspense and then finally Nikos's deep male tones came down the phone.

'Mariakos.'

'Nikos, I need you to see a child,' she said quickly, feeling the colour pour into her face. What if he snapped at her for disturbing him?

But he didn't.

He simply said 'I'll be right there,' and replaced the phone before she could respond.

'You're brave,' Kelly muttered. 'Girlfriend's prerogative, I suppose.'

'I'm not his girlfriend.' What was she? She didn't know. She was having his baby and soon everyone would know that, but…

Ella pushed the problem out of her mind. 'Send him to me when he arrives. I have a toddler with abdominal pain that I'm worried about.'

She returned to the cubicle to find the mother reading quietly to Harry.

Ella checked the child's temperature again. 'I've spoken to the consultant. He's on his way.'

'Will he yell at me?' Carol was looking anxious. 'I wish I hadn't come now. Harry hasn't cried or anything since you left the room. He looks fine, which is great, obviously but now I'm feeling like a fraud.'

'Why would you feel like a fraud?' Nikos strode into the room and Ella felt her heart flip as it always did whenever she saw him.

What had he done with the diamond ring?

His brief searing glance told her that they had unfinished business and her insides were suddenly caught in a turbulence that left her breathless.

'Sorry to disturb your meeting. This is Harry,' she said quickly, relieved that they had something else to focus on other than their relationship. 'He's been suffering from abdominal pain for two days, and Carol feels like a fraud because she has already seen the GP.'

Nikos washed his hands. 'And his diagnosis was…?'

Carol flushed. 'Tummy bug. He said only time would help. He also told me that I had to relax a bit about parenting and that I was overreacting. And maybe I am, but—'

'What is it about Harry that is making you uneasy?' Nikos's tone was gentle as he squatted down so that he was the same level as the child. 'Is it anything specific or just a feeling?'

'He's been having these screaming fits that last a few minutes and then…' Carol shrugged helplessly. 'The GP said they were probably just tantrums, but he looks as though he's in pain to me. He just isn't himself. Normally he's cheeky, lively and into everything. Now it's as if he just doesn't have the energy.'

'Give me details, from the beginning.'

'Well, he had a bit of a cold—I didn't really think anything of it to be honest, and then he started holding his stomach and moaning that it hurt. It seemed to only last a few minutes and then it would go and he carried on as if nothing had happened.'

Nikos questioned her about the child, and about the consultation she'd had with her own doctor.

'Did he examine Harry's stomach?'

'No. He said it was just a virus and that I should have waited until after the weekend to bring him back.' Carol's eyes filled again. 'So I took Harry home, but he looked so awful and all morning he's been getting worse. I didn't know what to do so I just thought I'd bring him here. I know you probably want to yell at me too…'

As if on cue, another toddler in the waiting room started to cry and Nikos winced.

'As you can hear, it's the children that do the yelling in this department.' His tone dry, he rose to his feet and closed the door of the cubicle. 'I want to examine Harry properly, Carol. Can you lift him onto the trolley for me? Ella, do we have any toys? Something to distract him?' His smile was disarming. 'Normally I have toys, but I have just come from a meeting with the hospital manager and I have never yet persuaded them to take play seriously.'

Ella fished a different car out of the box and then tried a puppet, but in the end no distraction was needed because Harry lay quietly on the trolley while Nikos gently examined his stomach. Watching his skilled, confident hands move gently over the toddler's tiny body, Ella felt some of the tension leave her. She had no doubt whatsoever that he'd be able to identify the problem.

He was a brilliant doctor.

Had he dismissed Carol? No. He'd taken her concerns really seriously.

'Temperature?'

'His temperature is normal.' Ella wondered if he was finding it as hard to concentrate as she was. 'Do you think it's a virus?'

He didn't answer for a moment, his expression thoughtful as he felt the toddler's abdomen with gentle fingers. 'No,' he said finally. 'I don't. The signs aren't classic, but…' his eyes narrowed thoughtfully as he studied the pale, listless child. 'I wonder…? Ella, ring Ed Green for me. Ask him to come down.'

Ed Green was the paediatric surgeon and Ella hurried

to the phone and made the call, wondering what was going through Nikos's mind.

Nikos was talking to Carol. 'You were right to bring him,' he said quietly, 'and to trust your instincts.'

Carol looked at him anxiously. 'It isn't a tummy bug?'

'No. Harry has something called intussusception.' He reached for a pen and a piece of paper and quickly drew a diagram. 'This is the bowel, yes? Sometimes one segment of the bowel can telescope into the next part—this is what we call intussusception.'

'And Harry is showing signs of that?'

'Actually no,' Nikos conceded, returning the pen to his pocket. 'He isn't showing any of the classic signs.'

'Then how do you know what it is?'

'I just know.' Nikos gave a ghost of a smile. 'You have maternal instincts that told you something was wrong, and I have instincts also. Doctor instincts. A gut feeling, I think you call it.'

'Is it something serious?'

'It can be,' Nikos said carefully, 'but in this case I think we have caught it early, thanks to those instincts of yours. My colleague is on his way now, and—'

'Nikos?' Ed, the paediatric surgeon, strode through the door, a slight man with glasses and sandy-coloured hair. 'What can I do for you?'

Nikos briefly outlined the history and Ed walked to the side of the trolley.

'Intussusception?' He checked the observation chart that Ella had completed.

'Harry is displaying none of the classic signs,' Nikos said in a cool tone. 'No temperature, a small amount of diarrhoea yesterday, but nothing since, one episode of vomiting and no abdominal mass.'

'So you're making an educated guess.' Ed examined the child's abdomen himself. 'Could be appendicitis.'

Nikos shook his head, confident and sure of himself. 'It's intussusception. And it's not a guess.'

Ed lifted an eyebrow, his gaze challenging. 'You can't be sure, Mariakos.'

Nikos met his gaze full on. 'I'm sure. As he's showing no signs of perforation, a barium enema is probably the most appropriate choice.' He walked away from the trolley and took Carol to one side. 'Mr Green is going to sort out the problem. And I will phone your GP.'

'Thank you so much.' She was tearfully grateful, visibly worried about Harry, and Nikos closed a strong brown hand over her shoulder in a gesture of support.

'It took great courage for you to come here, having already been told that he was fine,' he said softly. 'You were very brave and you have done Harry a great service because if the condition had been left too much longer, the outcome might not have been so good. You are an excellent mother and Harry is a lucky boy.'

Carol's cheeks grew pink but his words seemed to give her an extra boost of strength and she was calm as Harry was transferred into the care of the surgeons.

A few hours later Ella caught up with Nikos as he worked his way through the long queue of children waiting to be seen. Two more doctors had come over from the main emergency department to help, but it was Nikos who saw the difficult cases.

'Ed Green just called.'

Nikos looked up from the set of notes he was writing. 'How is Harry? Did Ed leave a message?'

'Yes.' Ella hesitated. 'He said to tell you that you're an arrogant Greek and one day you're probably going to fall flat on your handsome face, but in the meantime if either of his kids are ever brought into Paediatric Casualty, please can you make sure that you're on duty.'

Nikos smiled. 'I'll do my best.'

'He was telling you your diagnosis was correct.'

'I know it was correct. I was never in any doubt about that. But you are also responsible for the fact that the child is going to be all right.' He leaned back in his chair. 'You were right to call me out of that meeting. Well done.'

The praise lifted her spirits. 'Did you speak to the GP?'

'Yes.' With that economical answer, Nikos calmly rose to his feet. 'And now to an entirely different subject. You're not spending another night on that canal boat. I want you to move in with me. We will drive over to the boat after work and fetch your things.'

Stunned, Ella just looked at him. 'I'm not marrying you, Nikos. Didn't you listen to anything I said to you?'

'Yes. You said that you don't know me.' His tone was cool. 'So—move in with me and you will soon realise that I am exactly the same person with or without money. The money just means that someone else cooks our cheese on toast and we have more room in the bed.'

'It isn't that simple, Nikos! I can't possibly move in with you!' It was hard enough resisting temptation without living under the same roof as him. 'No.'

'We can fight about this if you wish.' Carefully, he put down his pen. 'But I will win.'

'No, you won't!'

His strong, confident hand rested briefly on her stomach. 'I'm the father, Ella,' he said softly. 'What are you going to tell him when he asks you why his parents are not together? How are you going to explain that?'

She closed her eyes and sucked in a breath. 'That's fighting dirty, Nikos.'

'Then don't fight me. I will do whatever it takes to get you to do the right thing for our child. You say that you don't know me, and maybe you don't because if you did then you would know that I would *never* let my child be brought up outside marriage. And now I've told you that about myself, I want to know something about you. Look at me.' His hand slid under her chin, tilting her face. 'I want to know why you are being so stubborn about this.'

'You know why,' she croaked, struggling to ignore the stroke of his fingers. 'You walked out on me. You ended our relationship. You chose to leave. The only reason you're here now is because of the baby and that isn't good enough for me. You haven't stayed with any woman for more than six months. You don't show commitment.'

He lifted an eyebrow. 'I'm prepared to marry you—that shows commitment.'

'What happens when you decide to move on? I'm protecting my baby, Nikos.'

'Our baby,' he said harshly, his hands caging her face. 'It's *our* baby, *agape mou*. And the role of protector is mine. I am the man, no? I am the one who goes hunting, who carries a spear and repels invaders. You can rely on me to protect our baby. That isn't something you need to worry about.'

Unless the threat to the baby came from him.

What happened when he got tired of her and moved on to another woman?

'You've regressed to caveman mode again,' she muttered, hating the fact that part of her responded to his ultra-traditional male views. 'You don't care about being politically correct, do you?'

'I care about what's best for our child.' Dark lashes shielded his expression as he watched her. 'What about you, Ella? What do you care about?'

'I also care about what's best for our child.'

'Then marry me and stop this nonsense.'

Ella pulled away from him, feeling as though she was suffocating.

He was *so* sure of himself. And the really cruel thing was that she wanted to say yes so badly.

She loved him and she really, *really* wanted to let him put the ring back on her finger and pull her into the fairy-tale life he was offering her.

But she didn't dare. If she made that leap, she'd fall.

And her baby would fall, too.

'I don't want to talk about this any more.' Tense, on edge, she backed towards the door. 'I'm living on my canal boat and that's final.'

His only reaction to her words was a tightening of his beautiful mouth. 'How many nights have you spent on that boat?'

It seemed like a strange question. 'Last night was the first one. But I don't see what that has to do with anything.'

He didn't answer. He simply looked at her for a long moment and then straightened and glanced at his watch. 'I'm due at the university—I'm giving a lecture to a bunch of medical students. I'll see you later.'

Ella opened her mouth to repeat that she wasn't going to move in with him but his long stride meant that he was already halfway down the corridor.

She stared after him in confusion, still wondering why he was interested in how many nights she'd spent on the boat.

What did that have to do with anything?

It didn't matter how many nights she'd spent on the boat. She wasn't going to change her mind and move in with him. How could she? *How could she ever risk that?*

Remembering what he'd said to her, her hand dropped to her abdomen.

'I'm doing it for you,' she whispered to the baby. 'He doesn't love me. He didn't choose to be with me. He's only here because of you. And that isn't good enough, is it? You wouldn't want that. Trust me. I know.'

Frustrated by Ella's determined refusal to marry him, Nikos strode towards his car, scrolling through his emails on his BlackBerry.

His mouth tightened impatiently as he ruthlessly deleted anything and everything that didn't grab his attention.

One email caught his eye and he scanned the contents.

Sliding behind the wheel of his car, he made a call. 'The house is all confirmed?' Listening to the stammering excuses of an incredibly starstruck estate agent, Nikos sighed. 'I don't want to wait a month. I want the house today. Give me the phone number of the family who own the house. I will speak to them myself.' Ignoring the man's feeble protests that he was paid to conduct negotiations on the property, Nikos skilfully extracted the number out of the man and then called the family who lived in the house.

The house he wanted.

It took him under two minutes to negotiate an outcome that was satisfactory to both parties and a further minute to make arrangements for the key to be delivered to the hospital. He placed one further call to Athens and then gave a satisfied smile.

The job was done.

He had a house. A house that she was going to love. She obviously wanted a slice of country living and he'd just bought her an *extremely* large slice. It was set in acres of grounds, which should satisfy Ella's need for a rural retreat, and it was right on the beach.

All he had to do now was persuade her that she was going to live in it.

And she was going to fight him all the way, of course, because she seemed determined to fight him about everything.

Reversing out of his space, Nikos tried again to work out what was going on in her head.

Was she really resisting his proposal simply because he hadn't divulged the details of his financial situation?

What difference did it make that he had money? Most women would have been delighted to discover that their future was secure. Particularly someone like Ella, who was obviously struggling by on a ridiculously tight budget.

But Ella didn't seem remotely interested in his money. Just in the fact that he hadn't told her about it.

He felt a rush of frustration because her reaction didn't make sense.

And then he experienced the same feeling that he always had when a sick baby was brought into the department. They couldn't tell him what was wrong and he loved the challenge of using all his skills to reveal the answer.

It would be the same with Ella, he vowed as he turned onto the road that led to the university. He was a doctor, wasn't he? He needed to take a step back. Be more objective. Examine the clues.

But the first step was to have her living under the same roof as him.

Exhausted after the end of a long shift, Ella changed into her jeans, slung her bag over her shoulder and said goodnight to the night staff who had just come on duty.

There was no sign of Nikos and that surprised her because she'd been braced for another argument about the unsuitability of living on a canal boat.

In the darkness outside in the ambulance bay, she fumbled with the lock on her bike and then wheeled it down the dark alleyway that led from the emergency department to the back of the hospital and the canal path.

It was the first time she'd seen the canal at night and cold fingers of unease trailed down her spine.

She'd been asleep when Nikos had carried her home the previous evening. Only now was she realising what it would be like to cycle home along this lonely path at night.

And as for sleeping on the boat on her own…

Suddenly she wished she hadn't been quite so quick to dismiss Helen and Nikos's concerns. Perhaps pregnancy had done strange things to her imagination, but she felt horribly, horribly uneasy, staring along the dark, lonely path.

Irritated with herself, she switched on the light at the front of her bike.

Looking at the sinister darkness that stretched ahead, Ella almost wished Nikos was there. His powerful shoulders and raw male strength would have done a great deal to calm her nerves.

Knowing him as she did, she was frankly a little shocked that he'd allowed her to cycle home without more of a fuss.

Swallowing hard, she stared into the shadowy darkness and felt another lurch of unease. What was the matter with her? This was what she wanted, wasn't it? She'd chosen to live here. She'd chosen peace and tranquillity. She'd wanted independence. Acknowledging the contradiction in her attitude, Ella sighed with frustration.

She accused him of being a caveman, so he let her cycle alone. And now she was wishing he'd been more forceful about stopping her.

Desperately, she tried to pull herself together. Really, she was being pathetic. She had a light on her bicycle so there was no chance that she was going to cycle into the canal. And as for everything else…

Refusing to examine any other fear, she pushed her foot down on the pedal and started along the path. The wheels of her bike crunched lightly on the rough ground and high in the trees an owl gave a ghostly hoot, reminding her that the surrounding woodland was very much alive at this time of night. Something gleamed between the branches of the trees—a pair of eyes?

Her heart was pounding, her hands were clammy and she was filled with a dark feeling that something, or someone, was watching her.

Her imagination racing out of control, Ella cycled faster than she should have done along the path, her shoulders prickling with the sense that someone was following her. Several times she was tempted to stop and look behind her, but instead she kept pedalling until she reached her boat.

Moments later she was safely inside, her bike propped against a tree outside, the doors locked against intruders.

Safe.

Trying to calm her breathing, she closed her eyes for a moment. She was locked in here. Everything was fine.

But still she couldn't relax.

Ridiculously nervous, she couldn't shake off the thought that no one else was close by. She had no neighbours. She was alone on a stretch of canal that was only used by dog walkers during the day.

Who used it at night?

Helen was right, she thought nervously, drawing the curtain across the windows so that no one could see inside. This place was too isolated.

Or maybe it was just her hormones that were making her this jumpy.

Irritated with herself, Ella made herself a cup of tea and picked up a pregnancy book. So far she hadn't even managed to find out what should be happening to her. *Perhaps she should start by looking in the index for something on hallucinations and delusions*, she thought dryly, embarrassed at how nervous she'd been cycling down that path.

Honestly, what an idiot she was.

And then she heard the distinct crunch of footsteps on the path that ran alongside the boat. It was a slow, heavy sound— a menacing crunch that definitely belonged to a man.

Ella ceased to breathe. The book slipped from her fingers and hot tea sloshed onto her leg.

She'd never known fear like it.

Someone was outside. Someone was standing there in the soft, velvety darkness, watching her.

And she had nowhere to hide.

Whoever it was *knew* that she was on the boat. That she was alone.

They'd followed her.

All the time she'd sensed someone behind her, she hadn't been paranoid...

There really had been someone there.

Watching.

Her heart pounded hard in her chest, her palms were suddenly damp and her mouth was dry. Reminding herself that the door was locked, Ella sat frozen to the spot, trying to convince herself that it was just someone walking their dog—ignoring the terrified part of herself that was telling her that people didn't generally walk their dogs at ten at night in total darkness.

The footsteps stopped and she knew, she just knew, that whoever had followed her was now standing directly outside her boat.

Her hand shaking, Ella fumbled in her bag for her mobile phone only to find that the battery was dead because she'd forgotten to recharge it.

She had absolutely no way of contacting anyone.

She was on her own.

Slowly, stiffly, she rose to her feet and closed her hand around a saucepan that was sitting on the top of the hob. It wasn't much of a weapon but it was the only thing she had.

And then she heard a thud and the boat rocked slightly as someone landed on the deck.

Her scream shattered the terrifying silence.

CHAPTER FIVE

PARALYSED with terror, Ella's hand tightened around the saucepan.

Her heart was pounding so hard it felt as though it was about to spring out from her chest.

And then she heard someone swear and a deep, male voice called her name. 'Ella?'

She was shaking so badly that it took a moment for her to realise that she recognised the voice.

Filled with relief, she tried to speak but instead she just burst into tears, all the pent-up tension exploding in a flood of emotion as she realised that the footsteps outside had belonged to Nikos, not an evil stalker.

'Ella!' His tone was savage. 'Let me in!'

She heard him let rip a stream of Greek and then the door crashed open and he forced his way into the cabin like a warrior going into battle.

'*Theos mou*, what has happened? Who has hurt you? Tell me!' His strong hands closed over her shoulders and Ella launched herself against his powerful chest. He braced his legs to steady them both, his arms closing round her protectively as she burst into sobs. 'Talk to me!'

Ella ignored his urgent command and clung to him, so relieved that he was there that she was totally unable to speak

He swore fluently in English, then switched to Greek as he scooped her up in his arms and sat with her cradled on his lap.

She didn't understand a word he was saying, but his deep, strong voice was so reassuringly male that she didn't care.

'Hush, now. Stop crying.' His hand infinitely gentle, he stroked her hair away from her face as if she were a child. 'Tell me what happened. What was it that frightened you?'

'I thought someone was following me—I heard someone and my phone was dead and there was this owl…' Babbling incoherently, Ella tried to explain, her fingers holding so tightly to his shirt that her knuckles were white.

'You live in the country so you will hear owls, no?' Carefully he extracted his shirt from her grip and took possession of her hand. 'And your phone is dead because you have always been useless at remembering to recharge it. And as for the person following you—' He broke off and muttered something under his breath.

'What? Did you hear someone when you were outside?'

The breath hissed through his teeth. 'The footsteps were mine, Ella.' His fingers tightened on hers. 'I was the one following you.'

She stared at him with incomprehension. 'You were following me? Why?'

'Because you are impossibly stubborn and you insist on living in this place in the middle of nowhere!' His dark gaze burned fiercely into hers. 'Did you really think I was going to let you cycle home alone? I was held up by a phone call and by the time I'd finished, you'd gone. I wanted to check that you were safe.'

'It was your footsteps I heard.'

'Yes.'

'I was terrified.'

'I'm sorry. Obviously the last thing I wanted to do was frighten you. But it does prove that you should *not* be living here alone,' he gritted, sliding his free hand into her hair and tilting her face to look at him. 'It is not a suitable place for a woman. Tonight has proved that.'

'That isn't true. It was you all along—'

'But it might not have been me.' His tone was edged with roughness. 'It might not have been me, and then what, Ella? You think a saucepan is going to be sufficient defence against an intruder? What were you going to do? Sauté him with garlic and serve him on a bed of pasta?'

'I was going to hit him, of course.' Stung by his sarcasm and increasingly embarrassed by the whole incident, Ella made a desperate attempt to regain some of her pride and dignity. 'It's possible that I overreacted,' she said stiffly, 'I think it's hormones or something. I was imagining all sorts of things. I'll be fine now.'

She just wanted to curl up in a ball and hide.

What a pathetic wimp she was!

What a spineless excuse for a twenty-first-century woman.

She'd made a *total* fool of herself. How on earth had she worked herself up into such a state?

Calm now in the safety of Nikos's lap, she glanced around her, wondering what it was about this cosy canal boat that had seemed so terrifying.

'You'll be fine? You're sure?' Nikos tipped her gently off his lap and onto the seat as he rose to his feet. 'In that case I will leave you to it. I know how badly you want to stay here on your own, so—'

'You're going to leave me?' Alarmed, disbelieving, Ella looked at him, her heart starting to race again. 'Y-you're *going*?' Without him there, the canal boat would cease to be cosy. She could feel the menace closing in around her— the dark trees, the glassy surface of the water.

'You don't want me here, I understand that. I never intended to come in—I just wanted to see that you arrived home safely.' His back to her, Nikos dropped into a squat and fiddled with the door. Then he picked up the key, performed some deft manoeuvre that she couldn't see and then rose to his feet. 'This lock is fine. It's not that secure, so miraculously it didn't actually break when I forced it. You can lock it again after I leave. You might want to sleep with that saucepan by your bed, just in case.'

The lock wasn't secure?

Fear and pride fought a quick, desperate battle for supremacy.

'Wait a minute—you can't leave.' Fear trampled on pride as she forced the words out. 'I don't want you to leave.'

'You don't?' He turned to look at her, his eyes glittering dark. 'Why?'

She swallowed. 'Because…I feel better when you're here.'

'I thought you liked living alone on the canal,' he said silkily, his sardonic tone dragging over her nerve endings, 'I thought this was your idea of blissful independence. I'd hate to get in the way of that.'

His powerful frame almost filled the boat and she knew that her sudden feeling of security came from his presence and nothing else.

If he left…

'I like having you here.'

One dark eyebrow lifted. 'As your bodyguard? You want my muscles, yes? My ability to throw a punch?'

The chemistry crackled between them, a powerful force drawing them together in the small, intimate space they both occupied.

Feeling the immediate reaction of her body, Ella felt herself weaken. 'Not just as my bodyguard.' Oh, dear God, what was she doing? *What was she saying?* It must be something to do with the darkness. 'I—I just don't want you to go.'

Nikos slowly and deliberately turned the key in the lock, securing the door from the inside. 'I'll stay,' he said softly, 'but only if you promise that tomorrow you'll move out of this place.'

Ella's heart was thudding. 'Nikos, I—'

'Do you want to spend tomorrow night alone here?'

'No.' She shook her head, hating herself for being so wimpy. 'It's gorgeous during the day. I love the water and the wildlife, but…it's spooky at night.'

What was the point of denying it?

Given her dramatic performance over the past few minutes he was only too aware of how spooky she found it. His shirt was still wet from her tears and he probably had scratch marks from where she'd clung to him for dear life.

He picked up the saucepan and returned it to the kitchen area, amusement in his dark eyes. 'We won't be needing that any more. If I am required to repel an intruder I would choose to use hand-to-hand combat rather than kitchen utensils.' Then he took her hand and pulled her gently to her feet. 'Time for bed, *agape mou*. You are exhausted and I am too tall for this boat. It will be more relaxing for both of us if we lie down.' Without giving her time to pass comment on that suggestion, he tugged her along the narrow passageway that led to the bedroom area.

Ella recoiled as she saw the insects. 'Oh, dear—I must have left the window open.' She eyed an enormous spider with horror and wondered if she dared ask him to remove it. But she'd already made such an utter fool of herself that this time pride was the stronger force and she remained silent. But she watched the spider, desperately willing it to find its own way to the window.

Nikos angled his glossy dark head and looked at her quizzically. 'I thought you liked the wildlife. Being close to nature.'

'Ducks,' Ella muttered. 'I like the ducks. And the dragonflies are pretty from a distance.'

To give him his due, he didn't tease her. He simply scooped the spider up in his palm and gently tipped it out of the window. 'Anything else?'

Ella's face was scarlet. He already knew she was a coward, so what was the point in pretending? 'The daddy-long-legs on the ceiling?'

Nikos rehoused the daddy-long-legs outside the boat and Ella gave a weak smile.

'OK. This is embarrassing. You think I'm completely pathetic.'

There was laughter in his eyes as he cupped her face in his hands. 'I think you are beautiful,' he said huskily, 'and you are all woman. I think perhaps a canal boat is not the best setting for you. You should be sharing luxurious surroundings with an over-protective Greek male, not a selection of British wildlife. You should be pampered and cosseted and spoiled.' He drew her T-shirt over her head in a decisive movement and then reached for the snap of her jeans.

As his warm fingers brushed against the sensitised skin of her stomach, a spasm of excitement shot through her and she gave a soft little gasp.

'No, honestly Nikos, we shouldn't do this. It will just confuse everything.'

'I'm not confused.' He gave a sexy, possessive smile. 'Your jeans are tight, *agape mou*. Soon this baby of ours will begin to show and people will ask questions.' He lowered his head and his mouth gently brushed that one sensitive place at the base of her throat. 'By the time that happens, you will be my wife.'

'Nikos—'

'We will spend the night here,' he purred, 'and I will protect you, no?'

There seemed little point in protesting that she could protect herself after her miserable performance so far, so she kept silent.

And suddenly she realised that the only really threatening thing left in the boat was him. *The way he made her feel.*

It felt as though there was a war going on in her head.

Dizzy with longing, Ella rested her forehead against his chest, breathing in his tantalising male scent, reminding herself of all the reasons she shouldn't be doing this. And then his strong hands slid down her bare arms, the slow, sensual slide of his flesh against hers a promise of things to come.

It was impossibly intimate, just the two of them in this small, enclosed space surrounded only by nature.

A raw, primal sound came from outside the boat and she gave a start. 'What was that?'

With soft laughter, he tipped her back onto the bed and came over her, his body powerful and protective. 'Foxes mating,' he breathed huskily, a smile touching the corners of his mouth as he gently brushed her face with his fingers. 'And now you need to block out the sounds you hear or by the morning you will be taking tranquillisers. You have no reason to be afraid of anything because I am here.'

Ella gasped as his clever fingers slid between her thighs and rested there, close to the part of her that was aching with longing.

It had been four months…

She shifted her hips slightly but he didn't move his hand. Instead his firm, sexy mouth glided onto hers with effortless skill and the sounds of the night outside faded out of her brain as excitement erupted inside her.

The first time he'd ever kissed her she'd decided that she could happily spend the rest of her life doing this one thing and never stop. And this time she had no reason to rethink that ambition. What Nikos could do to a woman's mouth was something that no female should die without experiencing.

The erotic slide of his tongue sent a fire burning low in her pelvis and she shifted against the sheets. His fingers rested at the top of her thigh, tantalisingly close to that part of her that ached and throbbed. But he didn't move his hand. Instead, he transferred his mouth from her lips to her breasts, teasing her jutting, sensitised nipples with the slow, relentless graze of his tongue. It was like completing an electric circuit. Sensation arced through her body, piercing her low in her pelvis. Ella lifted her hips in silent invitation but still his fingers didn't move—*didn't touch her where she most wanted to be touched.*

She gave a tiny gasp of frustration and desperation and when he drew the whole of her nipple into his warm mouth, that gasp turned to a moan and then a sob.

When exactly had he removed her panties?

The question flew into her head and out again because she was too dizzy and dazed to hold onto any coherent thought for long. Her body was on fire, her only focus to relieve the maddening ache that he had aroused in her.

'Nikos…'

But he ignored her whispered plea and instead turned his attention to her other breast while his clever, teasing fingers gently stroked the inside of her thigh, slowly driving her mad with longing.

He trailed his mouth down her body and lingered for a moment on her gently rounded flesh. 'My baby.'

His possessive tone set off an alarm bell in her head but Ella was too excited to pay attention. The ache in her pelvis was almost painful and her breath came in tiny gasps as she tried to snatch air into her starving lungs. The whole of her world was centred around his fingers—waiting, just waiting…

But in the end it wasn't his fingers that touched her first, it was his mouth.

With firm, determined hands he gently spread her thighs and settled his mouth on that single part of her which he'd so far delayed touching, and it felt so impossibly good that Ella cried out.

He gave her no opportunity to resist or be embarrassed because he identified his target with effortless accuracy, the relentless flick of his tongue so shockingly skilled that her fingers gripped the sheets in desperation.

He took her right to the very edge and held her there, trembling and shivering with expectation and anticipation and then he shifted over her, his eyes holding hers.

Barely able to breathe, Ella looked into his eyes and then

gasped as he gently slid his fingers deep inside the quivering softness that he'd created at the very heart of her. She moaned, knowing that she was close to exploding.

And he knew it too because he gently withdrew his fingers and shifted over her, and only then did she realise that he was naked, too.

Exactly how and when he'd removed the last of their clothes she didn't know. Neither did she care because she felt the roughness of his thigh brush against the softness of hers and then he slid a hand underneath her bottom, raising her slightly.

'You are exquisite,' he breathed, and then he entered her with a series of smooth, gliding thrusts that took him right to the very heart of her.

Her body exploded into an instant orgasm and she heard him swear under his breath as her body tightened around the powerful thrust of his arousal. He held himself still for a moment, teeth gritted, jaw hardened as he fought for control while she sobbed and clung to him. His hand scraped through her hair and he took her mouth, silencing her cries with his kiss, holding her hard against him as she tumbled and trembled in a sensual explosion that affected both of them.

Finally her body calmed and he groaned something in Greek against her mouth and then moved inside her again, the raw virility of his thrusts sending her spiralling out of control once more.

And this time she took him with her, the spasms of her body drawing a thickened groan from him as he surged into her with masculine force and then shuddered above her as he finally lost his iron grip on control.

It was primal, primitive and impossibly intimate and she

lay there struggling for breath, the palm of her hand pressed against his sleek, damp skin, her legs brushing against the hard muscle of his.

It was ages before either of them moved.

Finally, Nikos lifted his head, his breathing still uneven as he looked down at her. 'If you weren't already having my baby,' he said huskily, 'then you would be now.'

Her heart was still pounding. 'That's a really Greek male remark.'

'How many Greek males have you known?' His tone was rough but his eyes teased her. 'It is fortunate for you that I know you were very inexperienced when I met you.'

Frustrated by the effect he had on her, Ella stiffened defensively. 'I had boyfriends—' The rest of her sentence was cut off as he touched her mouth with his fingers.

'I don't want to know.'

'*Another* really Greek male remark.'

A faint gleam of mockery in his eyes, he rested his hand low on her stomach. 'Your body is changing.'

'You mean I'm fat.' She tried to keep her tone light but he was too experienced a doctor not to detect the thread of insecurity running through her glib comment.

'I am responsible for those changes…' his mouth brushed against hers '…and I love them.'

'Trust you to take it as a personal achievement.' Ella held her breath, desperately hoping that he might say something more than that in this cosy, intimate moment. *Something that might make her believe that this wasn't only about the baby.*

But he didn't. Instead, he angled his dark head as if he was listening to something outside.

'What? What have you heard?' She realised that it was

only his presence that was preventing her from having another panic attack.

'I was just thinking of the poor foxes,' he drawled softly, amusement in his eyes as he rolled onto his back and snuggled her against him. 'I can imagine the baby foxes saying to the mummy fox, "What are those noises?" And she will reply, "It's just humans."'

Ella giggled, but she was slightly shocked by the response he'd drawn from her. 'Do you think anyone heard us?'

'I sincerely hope not.' Nikos yawned and tightened his hold on her. 'Because if they did, it means that they are outside, listening, and you've done enough running around with a saucepan for one night. Relax. I am here. I won't let anything or anyone touch you or the baby.' With that arrogant assurance, he slid his hand down her body again, a wicked look in his eyes. 'Apart from me…'

Her body melted in instant response and she forgot about the world outside as he brought his mouth down on hers.

Ella woke to find herself wrapped around Nikos's bronzed, powerful frame.

Rain was thundering onto the roof of the boat and the ring was back on her finger.

She stared at the winking diamond in numb, disbelieving silence as she remembered all the things they'd done in the protective darkness of the night.

Dear God, she'd fallen into his arms like a terrified animal and he'd taken it from there, ruthlessly taking advantage of her vulnerability.

Swamped with horror and self-loathing, she sat upright and he opened his eyes, a question shimmering in those dark depths.

'Spider or daddy-long-legs?'

'Neither. It's you.' Clutching the sheet to her breasts, she slid away from him, averting her eyes from his mouthwatering body. 'You took advantage of me.'

'Did I?' He raised a dark brow. 'In what way did I take advantage of you?'

'I was scared and you—you…'

'I gave you the reassurance you needed.' He reached out a strong hand and pulled her back down beside him. 'Don't do this, *agape mou*. Don't start pretending that last night should never have happened. Just accept that it did. It was always going to happen. You wanted it and so did I.'

'No. No, I didn't.' She tried to pull away but he held her fast, moulding her body against his.

'Ella, you are having my child.' His hand was in her hair, his mouth a breath away from hers. '*Stop* fighting me because you know I will fight you back and I will win.'

This close, she couldn't think straight—she couldn't remember any of the reasons that this was a bad idea. She wanted him to kiss her again—*she wanted that so badly*. 'You're a bully.' But the words held no conviction and she watched helplessly as his sensual mouth curved into a slow smile.

Oh, dear God, she was a lost cause.

'I'm not a bully.' His voice was husky and amused at the same time. 'I just know what I want. And I know you want it too, but you're afraid. Why?'

'Because you're only here because of the baby.'

'What we just did had nothing to do with the baby.'

'That was sex. It isn't enough, Nikos.' Before she could change her mind, Ella tugged the ring off her finger and pressed it against his chest.

Rolling onto his back, he closed his eyes, apparently bored with the discussion. 'Every time you take that ring off your finger, I will put it back on again.'

Her body hummed with awareness and she knew that she had to get away from him before she made another bad decision. 'I need the bathroom.'

He released her reluctantly and Ella slid out of bed, pulling a fresh T-shirt from the case that she hadn't yet unpacked.

She stood in the tiny bathroom, knowing that she'd just made a hard situation even more difficult. Her body ached with delicious awareness and all she wanted to do was return to the bed and sample more of his raw male virility.

She closed her eyes for a moment, wondering why giving the ring back and leaving his bed hadn't felt like an easy decision.

How had she let things go so far?

Why hadn't she resisted?

But she'd never been able to resist him, had she?

She left the bathroom and walked towards the kitchen area. Rain streamed down the windows and the trees along the canal seemed greener than ever. It was indescribably beautiful and Ella wondered how on earth she could have been scared the night before.

Exasperated with herself, she reached for the kettle and then gave a tiny scream.

Instantly Nikos was by her side. 'What? What is wrong?' He followed her gaze and then grinned as he saw that five huge snails had crawled through the vent and were now slowly making their way down the window. 'Ah—more nature. I suppose it is the rain that has brought them out. They climbed up the bulrushes and in through the window.'

Looking at their fat shiny bodies and the silvery trail that led into the boat, Ella shuddered. 'They're disgusting.'

'They're all part of living on the river,' Nikos said mildly, and she closed her eyes, knowing that she didn't have what it took to spend another night out here.

'All right. You win. I'll find a bedsit in town.'

In the process of relocating the snails to the river bank through the open window, Nikos frowned. 'A what?'

'A bedsit. It's a room where you sleep, live.' Ella lit the gas and put the kettle on. 'You must know what a bedsit is. It's basically one room.'

'One room?' Nikos threw a sardonic glance around their surroundings. 'You are finding this too spacious? You would prefer to be a little more cramped, perhaps?'

'A bedsit is all I'm going to be able to afford,' she said irritably, wishing something would dent that cool confidence that she was finding increasingly infuriating.

'Ella, when I said that you shouldn't live here, I didn't intend that you should find somewhere else.' He gently dispatched the final snail on a new course. 'You're going to move in with me. And before you feel obliged to come up with a million objections, I ought to warn you that it's not negotiable. I'm willing to postpone the wedding until you've got used to the idea, but you're not spending another moment on this boat.'

Ella eyed the snails, now clinging to the dripping bulrushes. She looked at the overgrown path and the dark shadows that became even darker at night. And then she thought about how much trouble she'd had finding anywhere to rent at this time of year. 'All right.' Her tone was grudging. 'But just because I'm willing to stay with you for a few nights, it doesn't mean I'm saying yes to the rest of it. This is just temporary.'

She'd find somewhere of her own as soon as she could.

She wasn't going to let him push her into making a decision she'd regret.

'Of course it is temporary. We still need to have a discussion about where we will live permanently.' Nikos opened one of her cupboards, a frown on his face. 'Is there any food here? Get dressed. I'm taking you to your new home for breakfast.'

Ella turned the gas off, keeping one eye on the snails. 'We'd better stop at a shop on the way because there won't be any more food in your house than there is on this boat.'

'There will be food.' Nikos strolled back towards the bedroom area to retrieve his clothes. 'I have a chef, a housekeeper and a gardener, and if between them they can't manage to produce breakfast, they can search elsewhere for employment.'

Ella followed him down the passageway. 'You have staff?' She grabbed her jeans and tugged them on. Then she reached for her tiny suitcase and stuffed in the few items she'd got round to unpacking. 'How can you have staff when the house doesn't belong to you?'

'I brought my own staff with me.' He fastened his trousers and reached for his discarded shirt. 'They are part of the team who run my home on Crete.'

'You have a home on Crete?'

'Crete and Athens.' Deftly he fastened the buttons of his shirt and she glared at him.

'How can anyone live in two homes?'

'Crete is my real home. I still play a part in the family business so when I return to Athens I need somewhere that is mine.' He reached for his watch. 'I don't like hotels and, much as I love my family, I do not wish to stay within the smothering confines of their homes when I am in Greece. I need to be able to escape from their interference.'

'So where were you living when you were working in London?'

'In a hotel. It was simpler.'

'A *hotel*? I can't imagine what you must have thought, roughing it in hospital accommodation with me.'

He took her face in his hands and delivered a lingering kiss to her mouth. 'I thought that it was, without doubt, the best bed I had ever slept in,' he said huskily. 'And now stop being insecure. You wanted me to be honest with you, so I am being honest with you. Pack your things. We need to get some breakfast.'

CHAPTER SIX

NIKOS drove out of the city and down to the exclusive peninsula that boasted some of the most expensive, exclusive homes in England.

Ella's heart pounded as they approached that area.

Why here? Dear God, *why did it have to be here?*

But of course it would be here. He was a billionaire, wasn't he? And this was where the rich chose to live.

Should she say something?

Should she tell him exactly what this place meant to her?

Ella's fingers curled tightly around the edge of her seat and she told herself that there were several fantastic houses on this stretch of coast. It didn't have to be *that* one.

But it was.

Of course it was.

It was the best house in the area and it had direct access to the beach. Which other property would suit a Greek billionaire?

As Nikos parked the car at the end of the long, curving driveway Ella just stared. Her body felt strange as she contemplated her surroundings.

Fate, she thought bitterly. It was fate that he should bring her here. A test of how far she'd come.

Could she do it?

Could she live in this house that had played such a devastating role in her childhood?

She'd grown up looking at this house, staring at the outside and wondering about the inside. She'd pictured the whole place even though she'd never so much as peeped through a window.

'What's wrong?' Nikos switched off the engine, his expression questioning as he studied her face. 'You're very pale.'

'I'm fine.' Her mouth was dry, her heart pounding with anxiety. A small part of her wanted to blurt out the truth but confiding in anyone was so alien to her that the words never reached her mouth.

'I'm a doctor, Ella.' He lifted his hand and rubbed her cheek gently with the backs of his fingers. 'I can see that something is wrong. Tell me.'

The affectionate gesture brought a lump to her throat. Knowing that he wasn't going to let it go unless she gave him an explanation, she told a half-truth. 'Helen and I sometimes played on this beach as children and we always looked at this house. We used to dream up stories about the people who lived here.' *It was sort of the truth*, she thought numbly, her eyes on the huge glass windows that were designed to catch every ray of light.

'Well, now it's your home.' He switched off the engine. 'And it will remain your home until we are married. Then we'll decide where we are going to base ourselves.'

Feeling as though life was running away from her, Ella stared at the house. If ever she needed something to remind her that she couldn't marry him, it was this place.

Because this house, with its air of pampered luxury, reminded her of man's weakness.

She opened the car door, drawn to the house by a masochistic drive that she didn't understand. Part of her wanted to tell him that she just couldn't live here but another part of her was dying to look inside. How many hours had she spent wondering? Picturing what it was like.

She wanted to see. She wanted to stop imagining and *know.*

'Do they let you in wearing jeans?' She made the joke to divert attention from her reaction but she knew from his keen gaze that it hadn't worked.

He knew something was wrong.

Wishing he wasn't so astute, she rubbed her hands over her jeans. 'Perhaps I'll go shopping.'

'I will take you shopping. It will fit nicely with a commitment I have in London. In the meantime, I'll show you around.'

Rather than using the front door, Nikos guided her round to the back of the house, which faced the beach. Taking her hand firmly in his, he led her up the steps that led to the terrace.

Ella stood for a moment, almost expecting to feel a hand on her shoulder removing her for being an impostor.

From this privileged position on the cool wooden deck she had a view over the whole beach and she watched the families crowded together, playing on the sand.

'Tell me what you're thinking.' His voice was soft and Ella kept her eyes on the beach because a tiny part of her wanted to tell him everything.

But that tiny part was firmly embedded under the barriers she'd erected to keep everyone away from her vulnerabilities. 'I sat and dug in that very same spot, with Helen. We were eight years old.'

And she hadn't been able to stop crying.

Her view of the world had been damaged forever.

Relationships were as fragile as sandcastles, she thought bleakly, staring at a child on the beach piling sand into a bucket and then tipping it out. Full of hope and expectations, you built something. And it took so little to knock it down.

'You lived here as a child?'

'No. I lived ten miles down the road.' In a cramped one-bedroom flat that had been as different from this house as Africa was from Antarctica.

'Do your parents still live locally? You've never talked about them.'

'You never asked. Talking wasn't part of our relationship, was it?'

'I'm asking now.'

She gave the answer she always gave. The answer she'd memorised decades before. 'My parents separated when I was young. Dad went abroad. We're not in touch any more. Then my Mum died and I went and lived with Helen. I was lucky. They took me in.' She was quite proud of the fact that she'd managed to make her childhood sound like something ordinary. *Something that a million children might have experienced.* Sure that she had a tight grip on her emotions, she was even confident enough to elaborate. 'Helen used to build these fantastic castles. Moats, drawbridges, battlements— and then she'd work out ways that the prince was going to arrive and take her away to happy-ever-after land.' The breeze was picking up and Ella rubbed her bare arms gently.

'And you?' He pulled her against him, warming her. 'What was your prince going to do?'

'I was much too realistic to think about princes.' She felt the strength of him and the temptation to cling was so great that she had to force herself to pull away. Strolling forward to the edge of the terrace, she felt her knees shake. 'I ought to unpack and get changed for work. Can I…?' Her voice cracked. 'Would you mind if I found my own way around?' It would be easier that way. She wasn't sure she could trust her reactions and at least this way she knew there wouldn't be any witnesses.

He was frowning slightly, but he didn't argue. 'Go ahead. Take a shower and change and I'll meet you out here for something to eat when you're ready.'

Ella walked slowly towards the house feeling the same way she'd felt when she'd been eight years old.

Vulnerable. Exposed.

Hands clammy, heart out of control, she paused in the doorway and then inhaled deeply and stepped into her past.

Nikos stood on the terrace with his back to the beach, his fingers tapping an impatient rhythm on his thigh as he watched her enter the house.

Why did she want to look around the house on her own?

Was she insecure about the size of it?

Did she feel as though she didn't belong?

Was this about the money?

Pondering that question, Nikos strolled after her.

Light poured through the soaring windows, emphasising the space and luxury. Nikos admitted to himself that he'd expected a more enthusiastic response from her.

Avoiding the master bedroom suite, he showered and shaved and then walked back onto the terrace to find Ella already there. She was standing by the railings that skirted the terrace, staring down at the beach that stretched into the distance.

In a single glance, Nikos admired her long, fabulous legs and the curve of her hips. She'd changed into a pair of linen shorts that stopped at mid-thigh, and her simple strap top was made decent by the sleek fall of her blonde hair.

But he had a feeling she'd dressed without thinking.

She didn't seem aware of his presence and Nikos moved closer, his eyes drawn to the white peaks of her knuckles. She was gripping the railings as if trying to stop herself falling into a deep chasm.

Nikos felt a flash of concern, followed by frustration.

She was blocking him out.

On the other hand, he'd ended their relationship, hadn't he?

His mouth twisted into a smile of self-mockery. What did he expect? Earning trust wasn't that simple. It was going to take a while for her to trust him.

Acknowledging the similarities between them, he approached her and gently eased her hand off the railings and into his. Her fingers were cold and stiff. 'Did you find everything you needed?' He rubbed gently, warming and relaxing her hands with his.

'Yes, thank you. It's very comfortable.'

She looked as though she'd suffered a shock or a major trauma and he wished he could read her mind.

Normally women just spilled out problems without prompting but Ella's mind seemed to be like a password-protected computer program. There was no access to unauthorised users.

Frustrated that she was shutting him out, Nikos gripped her arms firmly and turned her to face him. 'Tell me what's wrong.'

Her eyes lifted to his. Sea-green eyes, swimming with secrets. 'The last two days have been pretty stressful,' she croaked. 'I wasn't expecting to see you again, and suddenly here you are, waving a ring at me, and nothing is the way I thought it was.'

It sounded logical, and yet Nikos knew it wasn't the whole truth.

They stared at each other for a moment and then he released her, reminding himself of the value of patience.

'We should eat. We're due at the hospital soon.'

His staff had laid a table for breakfast and he poured her a glass of freshly squeezed juice, analysing the situation with cold objectivity. Sensing that to demand that she confide in him would achieve nothing except withdrawal on her part, he kept the conversation light.

'What do you eat for breakfast? My staff can cook eggs in any form you like. Bacon? Sausages? Just tell me.'

'Juice will be fine. I'm not that hungry.' Ella pulled out one of the chairs and sat with her back to the house. 'I—I think perhaps I'll just have something later.'

Was she worried about the baby? The wedding? Their relationship?

Nikos drizzled golden honey onto thick creamy yoghurt and placed the bowl in front of her. 'Eat,' he said gently. 'You can't work a whole shift on an empty stomach.'

Her fingers reached for a spoon. Toyed with it. In the end she managed three mouthfuls, but Nikos let it pass, making a mental note to make sure she ate in her tea-break.

The last two days had been a dramatic white-knuckle ride of emotions. He'd give her a couple of days, and then, if things hadn't settled down, he'd deal with it.

* * *

Her head throbbed, her heart ached and Ella felt as though she was going to fall apart.

The past week had been a nightmare.

It was that house, she thought miserably as she tried to bring some order to the chaos of the waiting room. *That stupid, horrid house.*

Every night she lay there wide awake, her mind in constant turmoil.

It was as if she'd been transported back to her childhood and it was clear to her now that she couldn't stay there any longer.

She couldn't spend another night in that place.

Exhausted and vowing to ring a letting agency in her break, Ella tidied a pile of magazines, threw toys back into the box and collected pages of discarded colouring.

'Help me! Someone, help me!' A young man shouldered open the door of the department, a toddler cradled in his arms. 'She's stopped breathing!'

Dropping the pages in her hand, Ella didn't hesitate. 'Bring her into Resus with me quickly.' She pushed open the doors and called to Kelly, who was taking patient details at Reception. 'Call Nikos—now.'

The man's movements were jerky and panicky and the child lay in his arms, limp and lifeless. 'We were eating our picnic on the beach and suddenly she just started to cough and then she was gagging as though she wanted to be sick but she wasn't and now she isn't breathing. Oh, God, do something!'

'Lay her on the trolley—that's right.' Ella opened the child's mouth to see if she could see anything obvious obstructing the breathing. 'Do you know what she was eating?'

'What were we eating? I don't know. I don't know.'

The man jabbed his fingers into his hair, struggling to think—so distraught he could barely speak. 'She was just— I don't know what was there, I can't even remember. Crisps. Bread. Sausages.' He put his hand on his forehead, almost out of his mind with worry. 'All the usual stuff.'

With the aid of a light, Ella examined the child's airway and saw a brownish lump lodged in the back of her throat.

Swiftly she weighed up her options.

She could attempt to remove the obstruction with a finger sweep, but there was always the chance that such a manoeuvre might push the object further down the child's throat. The alternative was to wait for a doctor who would use the laryngoscope and a pair of Magill's forceps.

'Don't let her die. Please, don't let her die.' The little girl's father had his hands in his hair, almost beside himself with fear and worry. 'I can't believe this is happening. Do something! Please!'

Aware that each moment counted and confident that the obstruction was within her reach, Ella used a single finger sweep in an attempt to clear the child's airway. The hard lump of food was driven forward by her finger and she carefully removed it from the child's mouth and placed it in a kidney dish.

Satisfaction rushed through her, to be followed swiftly by concern because the child still wasn't breathing.

Ella opened the child's airway and gave five rescue breaths just as Nikos strode into the room.

Prepared to start chest compressions, Ella opened her mouth to give him the history just as the child gave a choked cough and drew in a shuddering breath.

'Oh, thank God!' The father pressed his fingers to his

eyes and Nikos tilted his glossy dark head and gave Ella a faint smile.

'It seems as though I'm not needed after all.'

'I wouldn't say that,' she muttered, reaching for an oxygen mask and slipping it over the child's mouth and nose. 'Let's just say we started without you.'

The father was murmuring to his daughter—kissing her forehead. 'You're all right, baby. Daddy's here. Daddy's here.' He lifted his head and looked at Ella, his hand still stroking his daughter's curls. 'I don't know what to say. You were amazing—you didn't hesitate. You just…took over and sorted it.' Clearly overwhelmed, the father wiped his eyes and shook his head. 'Sorry—I'm so embarrassed…'

'Don't be.' Nikos closed a hand over the man's shoulder and then focused on the little girl. He examined her carefully, satisfying himself that all was well and that she was recovering.

'It was this.' Ella picked up the dish. 'Looks like one of those mini-sausages.'

'You did a finger sweep?'

'Yes. Are you going to tell me off for taking a risk?'

Nikos hooked his stethoscope round his neck, a sardonic gleam in his eyes. 'Why would I do that? Presumably you looked and decided that there was a good chance you could clear it. I call it a bold, decisive action rather than risk-taking.'

And that was his own approach, of course.

No one could ever accuse Nikos Mariakos of dithering.

'She seems fine now,' Nikos said to the father, 'but I'd like her to stay here for another hour, just to be safe. When she recovers a bit you can take her into the waiting room and let her play with the toys.'

'I can't thank you enough.' He stepped towards Ella and took her hands. 'Thank you.'

'You're welcome. I'm pleased she's OK.' Ella blinked, moved by the emotion in the man's face.

This father loved his child.

Scooping the little girl into his arms, he hugged her tightly. 'Don't ever scare me like that again.' He looked at Ella over the child's head. 'I think I've aged a million years in five minutes. You don't know what worry is until you have kids, do you? Could someone just pop outside and tell my wife everything is OK? She's pacing outside in the car park with the baby. She's just hopeless if one of them is ill or hurt, so I always take over. But I'm useless at it, too.'

'You're not useless.' Ella had tears in her eyes, too, and it was Nikos who reassured the man and led him back out to Reception.

She understood now why he was so good with the parents.

He'd been that parent.

What had happened to his daughter?

Ella's gaze flickered to the computer on the desk. She could look it up on the internet, but somehow that just didn't feel right. She didn't want to have to find out the details of his life from cyberspace. She wanted him to tell her.

She wanted him to trust her.

He'd lost a child and suddenly the enormity of that sank home.

And she was planning to take another child from him.

Guilt mixed with all the other emotions swirling in her head.

Did she have a right to deny Nikos a life with his child? Was she really protecting the baby, or was she protecting herself?

She dug her hands into her hair, tortured by indecision.

At that moment Nikos strode back into the room, his eyes narrowing as he saw her stricken expression.

'What's wrong?'

Ella looked at him helplessly, wishing men came with an instruction booklet and a guarantee. She wanted to take that leap, but she was just too frightened of it all going wrong. 'Nothing. I'm fine.'

Nikos pushed the door closed, giving them privacy. 'Don't tell me "nothing", Ella.' His accent was more pronounced than usual and she sensed the depth of his exasperation. 'You are very tired. You are working too hard.'

'I love my work.'

'You are an exceptional nurse.' He strolled across to her and took her face in his hands, his fingers gentle. 'But you have your own health to think about, too. Today you're finishing work at four o'clock.'

Ella froze. She didn't want to finish early. The thought of going back to the house made her heart race and her breathing quicken. She honestly couldn't do it. She needed to find somewhere else to stay tonight. 'I'm on a late,' she said firmly. 'I don't finish until nine. And I thought I might go for a drink with the others. It's Friday. We usually go out on Fridays.'

'Ella, you have been working twelve-hour days to get this department up and running.' Nikos trailed his fingers down her throat. 'You need a rest. Both of us have the weekend off—it makes sense to leave at four.'

His touch was driving her crazy.

Suddenly she wanted nothing more than an afternoon in bed with him—*but not if that bed was in the house on the beach.*

'I couldn't possibly ask Rose if I can leave early.' She didn't want to leave early. She didn't want to spend any more time at the house than was strictly necessary.

'Rose has already agreed. She's got cover for you.'

'Oh…' Running out of excuses, Ella bit her lip and searched for some plausible reason not to return to the house.

Nikos glanced at the clock on the wall. 'If we leave at four, you'll have time to enjoy the hotel this evening.'

'Hotel?' Ella stared at him blankly, wondering if she'd misheard. 'What hotel?'

'I mentioned it to you last week.' Nikos frowned, and it was obvious that he'd expected her to remember. 'I have business commitments in London this weekend. I thought we could combine it with some relaxation and shopping.'

London? 'We're not going back to the house?'

'No. My plan is to go straight to London. You can buy whatever you need when you're there.'

Ella felt weak with relief. She thought about the sheer indulgent luxury of staying in an anonymous hotel. No spooky, spider-ridden canal boat. No sleeping in *that* house, surrounded by hideous memories, afraid that her emotions might spill out at any moment.

Instead, she could relax in an anonymous hotel room that didn't remind her of anything and just think. Long baths, maybe a bit of shopping. Nothing threatening.

And two days in which to plan the best way to bring up the subject of finding alternative accommodation.

'Great.' She smiled brightly. 'I can't wait.'

Nikos spread his hands, visibly perplexed by her sudden change of heart. 'I thought you didn't want to leave the department.'

'Well, if it's all right with Rose, it's all right with me.'

She didn't care what she did as long as she didn't have to spend another night in the house.

Ella sat in the helicopter, feeling dazed. 'We're flying to London?' When they'd set out in the sports car, she'd assumed they'd be driving all the way, but Nikos had only driven as far as the nearest airport.

'This is a billionaire solution to Friday-night traffic.' Nikos fastened her seat belt. 'I have some urgent business in London and I don't have time to spend five hours stuck in stationary traffic.' He adjusted the strap to his satisfaction, his face close to hers, his rough jaw grazing her cheek.

She lifted a hand and stroked it into his hair. 'Are you trying to impress me or something?'

His smile was slow and wicked. 'I thought I'd already done that but I'm more than happy to impress you again when we arrive at the hotel.'

'Very funny.' Ella felt her heart flip. 'If you're going to London on business, why are you taking me with you?'

'Because you want to know about my life, and this is part of my life.' He delivered a lingering kiss to her mouth and then straightened. 'Tonight you can rest, and tomorrow we will enjoy ourselves.'

Intensely relieved to be spared a weekend at the house, Ella leaned her head against the seat and looked at him. 'All right. So what happens now? You give your instructions to your pilot or something?'

'I am the pilot.'

'*You're* going to fly this thing?' She felt a moment of alarm. 'Do you know how?'

'You think I'd be flying it if I didn't?'

'I don't know—you have been known to take risks.'

He grinned. 'So have you, *agape mou*. But I promise not to take risks when I'm in the air.'

Hoping that he was as good at that as he was at medicine, Ella gripped her seat. As the helicopter rose from the ground she held her breath and then let out a bubble of laughter because it felt wonderful to be in the air. As they flew over the beautiful English countryside, she found herself fascinated by the patchwork of green fields spread beneath her like a giant bedspread.

As soon as they landed, they were transferred by chauffeur-driven car to one of the most prestigious hotels in London.

Watching in awe as a Hollywood actress sailed past surrounded by her entourage, Ella rubbed her hands self-consciously over her jeans.

'I feel as though any moment now someone is going to order me to use the tradesman's entrance. I can't stay here.' She gave a helpless shrug, wondering what it was that he saw in her. 'I don't fit. I'm wearing the wrong things.'

'You're far more beautiful than any of their other guests.' Ignoring her insecurities, Nikos urged her gently across the opulent marble foyer. 'And the hotel staff are interested in my wallet, not in your wardrobe.'

'Exactly how big is your wallet?'

'Big enough to ensure that they smile when my fiancée arrives wearing ancient jeans.'

They were intercepted by a man in a suit who greeted Nikos so effusively that Ella assumed that they must be somehow related.

A brief conversation was followed by some frantic hand signals and then they were escorted up a flight of stairs, along a thickly carpeted corridor and into a series of rooms about four times bigger than any flat she'd ever lived in.

Ella stood in the doorway, glancing around her in disbelief.

'I booked us a suite.' Nikos pressed a note into the man's hand and he discreetly melted away, leaving the two of them alone. 'We'll have more room.'

'That guy at Reception—he was obviously thrilled to see you. Are you related?'

'He's the manager of the hotel.' Nikos slung his jacket over the nearest chair and glanced at his watch. 'I have twenty minutes to shower, change and get to my meeting. I'm sorry to abandon you. Will you be all right here by yourself for a few hours?'

'Of course.' Ella decided that she could happily spend the rest of her life living in this hotel suite. No insects, no cleaning. Noticing the giant plasma screen on one of the walls, she decided that a long, indulgent bath would be followed by channel flicking. 'Is there a map or anything?'

'Of London?' Already in the process of unbuttoning his shirt, Nikos frowned. 'I don't think you should go out.'

'I'm not going out. I wondered if there is a map of this suite.' Ella was laughing. 'I'm worried I might get lost finding my way around. Which of the many bedrooms am I supposed to sleep in?'

'Mine,' Nikos said silkily, his glance unmistakably sexual as he yanked off his shirt and exposed sleek, muscular shoulders.

Their eyes met.

Her smile faded and her heart thundered like hooves in a stampede.

The chemistry between them was hot, powerful and undeniable, and she licked her lips, wishing he wasn't going out in twenty minutes. She stepped towards him and he lifted a hand and gave a self-deprecating laugh.

'If I do what you want me to do, *agape mou*,' he breathed, 'I will miss my meeting and neither of us will get any sleep for the rest of the night. And you need rest. You are tired and emotional and tomorrow I want to take you shopping and have fun.'

'Oh.' Ella wrapped her arms around her waist, trying to calm the insistent buzz of her nerve endings.

'Don't look at me like that.' His tone dry, he walked towards the far end of the suite. 'I'm going to take a shower. An extremely cold shower.'

'*Kalimera*. Good morning.' Freshly shaved and dressed in black jeans and a casual shirt, Nikos joined Ella at the breakfast table.

He was so beautiful, she thought helplessly. What woman in her right mind would be able to resist a man like him?

For the first time in a week she'd slept soundly and she felt much better for it. No bad dreams. No bad memories.

'Did you come to bed last night?'

'I came in late and you were sound asleep. I didn't want to wake you and I had work to do.' He poured himself a coffee and glanced out of the window. 'It's a sunny day.'

'No slugs climbing up the windows?'

'You pay extra for slugs.'

'How do you know the manager so well?'

'This is where I lived when I was working in London. Why are you staring?'

'Because normal people don't live in hotels, Nikos,' Ella said faintly. 'They stay for a few nights.'

'I was working long hours.' He gave a careless shrug, as if that explained everything. 'Are you eating?'

'I had a croissant. So until you met me and suddenly decided that you preferred a narrow bed in the hospital, you lived here?'

'Yes.'

'Well…' She glanced around her with a rueful smile. 'Now I understand why you preferred to stay with me. Anything would be better than slumming it here. It must have been tough for you, coming back here after being squashed with me on a mattress designed for one.'

'The nights I spent with you were infinitely more pleasurable than anything a hotel suite can offer,' Nikos said softly, and she blushed, watching as his long fingers skilfully dissected an orange.

'So now I know why you're the manager's best friend.'

'It isn't entirely due to my contribution to his profits.' Nikos put the fruit on her plate. 'He has a nephew who had an accident while I was on duty.'

'How badly was he hurt?'

'He lived. Do you want something else to eat?'

'In other words, you saved him?'

Nikos shrugged. 'I was lucky.'

'No.' Her stomach flipped. 'You're a brilliant doctor, Nikos. I've always known that.'

But would he be a good father?

He didn't love her and yet he was obviously prepared to make a commitment to her and the baby.

Was it enough?

His eyes held hers for a moment. 'Today you have a major decision to make.'

Ella's heart thudded. He'd promised not to push the subject of marriage. 'Nikos—'

'You need to decide whether you want to go to the clothes, or whether you want the clothes to come to you.'

Ella gave a nervous giggle, relieved that he hadn't been talking about marriage. *She wasn't ready to tackle that subject again yet.* 'You mean you actually pick up the phone and someone delivers a load of clothes to your hotel suite? That happens in real life? You say, "She's about the size of a baby elephant," and they say, "We will bring you our finest selection suitable for baby elephants, sir."'

'You are not the size of a baby elephant.' Nikos leaned forward and poured himself another cup of coffee. 'And we can arrange for them to come here, if that is what you would prefer. But I thought you might enjoy choosing.'

'Choosing what?' Ella gave a helpless shrug. 'What do I need, Nikos? I don't go anywhere. And I don't have the money to blow on clothes. I need to find somewhere new to live and it's going to cost more than the canal boat and—'

'Good decision. We'll go out.' Supremely confident, he stood up and gently pulled her to her feet.

'I can't spend your money.'

'Then I'll help you,' he said calmly, a smile in his eyes. 'With practice and a little encouragement, I'm sure you can manage it.'

'I don't need clothes. I don't go anywhere.'

He hesitated and then took her face in his hands. 'You are going to be my wife. And I'm not sure that you will enjoy everything that that entails. Yes, sometimes we can spend our evenings on the terrace, sharing a bottle of wine when the baby is asleep, but sometimes we have to attend social functions.'

'What social functions?'

'Elegant social functions.'

'You mean like red-carpet stuff?'

'Yes. Sometimes. I am a doctor, but I'm also the patron of several charities that are important to me. On top of that I have a duty to my family to play a part in the business.'

'I'm not sure I'll be any good at that sort of thing. Even with an unlimited budget I don't think I can look elegant, Nikos. I'm a nurse.' Thinking of the pictures she'd seen in glossy magazines, she felt a sudden lurch of insecurity. 'I'm used to running round a hospital in scrubs, interacting with people who are usually under the age of ten.'

'Then tonight will be a pleasant change for you,' he said smoothly. 'You are coming with me to a very glittery, high-profile charity ball.'

Ella felt a mixture of excitement and trepidation. 'What if I let you down?'

'You won't let me down. You'll enjoy it. It is a perfect opportunity to dress up. A very glamorous event.'

Ella quailed. *She was definitely going to embarrass him.* 'I don't know how to be glamorous. Nikos, I work with children. My idea of smartening up is to put on a clean scrub suit.'

He stroked her hair away from her face. 'You will be beautiful, *agape mou*. Stop worrying.'

'What is the charity?'

Nikos described the work that the charity did in supporting families with sick children. 'The aim is to build another centre, where the children can go on holiday.'

'So the aim is to make money. I don't understand how they make money from a ball. Are the tickets expensive?'

'Very. But most of the fundraising goes on during the

evening. The organisers will auction prizes and generally find ways to persuade the guests to part with their money.'

'What if people can't afford much?'

'Then they're not invited,' Nikos drawled, pulling her against him. 'You will be spending my money, *agape mou*, not your own.'

'Who did you take last year?'

'My sister,' he said dryly, 'and we argued all evening. It is not an experience I intend to repeat.'

'I've never been to a ball,' Ella confessed. 'They always do a ballot for the hospital ball and I've never won. Not that I could afford the ticket even if I did win. And I wouldn't know what to do when I got there.'

Nikos gave her a curious look. 'The general idea is to have a nice time,' he said in a mild tone. 'It's considered entertainment. Along with the whole shoes, hair, dress thing that women seem to love so much. Enough talking.'

He took her to one of the top department stores and turned her over to the care of a sleek, groomed woman whose sole purpose in life seemed to be to drain Nikos's bank account in a single shopping spree.

Trousers, dresses, jackets and shoes, shoes, shoes— shoes with high heels, shoes with ribbons and bows, pink shoes, gold shoes—silk bags and boxes lined the floor.

Ella tried on what felt like the entire contents of the store and after about five minutes the girl abandoned her stiff reserve and opened up.

'So you're going to the ball tonight,' the girl murmured enviously, leaning forward to adjust the lie of a dress. 'Lucky you.'

'Do you think so?' Ella turned sideways to look in the mirror. 'What do you think of this?'

'I think I envy you,' the girl said dreamily. 'I'd give just about anything for one night with Nikos Mariakos.'

Ella felt her stomach lurch. 'You know him?'

'Of course. He's rich, eligible and gorgeous. His brother shops here, and his sister. That dress is too tight at the waist.' She frowned for a moment and then looked at Ella with dawning understanding. 'Are you…?'

'Eating too many doughnuts,' Ella said quickly, sensing that Nikos wouldn't want her pregnancy confirmed.

'Right, well, that sort of waist isn't going to work on you, but I think I have something else. It has two tiny straps made from crystals—not cheap, but that's not going to bother anyone with Mariakos as their surname.'

In the end Ella came away with an entire new wardrobe and although she tried to apologise frantically for the amount she'd spent, Nikos didn't seem remotely interested in the details.

'Did you find something to wear tonight?'

Thinking of the gorgeous dress that she'd fallen in love with, Ella smiled. 'Yes.' And she was excited about wearing it. And the shoes. And then she remembered the girl. 'I think she guessed I was pregnant. I tried saying that I'd just put on some weight but she didn't look convinced.'

Nikos's mouth tightened. '*Theos mou*, it hadn't occurred to me that she might notice. It will upset my family greatly if news of your pregnancy reaches the press before news of our engagement.'

'Are you sure they'd care?' It was an alien concept for Ella. He looked at her thoughtfully.

'They would care. They are very old-fashioned. And very eager to meet you.'

'They know about me?' Ella shrank at the thought. 'You've told them about the baby?'

'Of course. I am going to be a father. Naturally, this is something that I would share with my family. It is a cause for celebration, not apology.' He frowned and drew her towards him. 'Why would you be surprised about that?'

'I don't know. I suppose I didn't realise that you're that close to your family.' It was an alien concept to her.

'We're Greek,' he said, as if that explained everything. 'Greeks argue and interfere with each other, but families stick together.'

Ella thought of her own brief experience of family life. She thought of her fractured, twisted, grossly dysfunctional family unit.

It was so different from the model he described.

She found herself thinking about the picture he'd painted of a noisy, interfering extended family and wondering what it would be like to be part of something like that.

She really had no idea.

CHAPTER SEVEN

NIKOS paced the length of the suite, waiting for Ella to come out of the room. She'd been in there for hours, he thought grimly, glancing at his watch. What the hell was she doing? He'd arranged for the hairdresser to come to the suite so she hadn't had to do that herself.

How long did it take to pull on a dress?

It crossed his mind that she might have tied the sheets together and escaped out of the window.

With a flash of exasperation he rubbed the tips of his fingers over his forehead.

Tonight he was going to break down those barriers, he promised himself. By the end of the evening, she was going to be wearing his ring.

'Nikos?' Her voice was hesitant and he turned sharply to see her standing there, barely recognisable as the sweet, competent nurse he was used to seeing dressed in theatre scrubs or faded jeans.

Her blonde hair had been swept up in a modern style and a sheath of silver fell from two glittering straps to pool on the floor.

Feeling an explosion of sexual attraction, Nikos trailed his eyes down her trembling frame, fully intending to scrutinise every shimmering centimetre of her lush body. But his eyes refused to move from the creamy curves of her breasts, partially revealed by the gentle dip at the front of the dress.

Contemplating the full glory of her amazing body, Nikos almost swallowed his tongue.

'Can you please say something nice?' She gave an awkward shrug as she looked down at herself. 'You're making me nervous. You hate it, right? I look like something that fell off a Christmas tree. It isn't me, is it? I should have just chosen something that was plain black and safe...'

Nikos tried to answer, but every neurone in his brain appeared to have fused.

The only coherent thought in his head was that they were going to miss the ball.

'Nikos?'

He gave up on speech. Instead, he crossed the room in two strides, hauled her hard against his ferociously aroused body and brought his mouth down on hers.

Her lips parted under the pressure of his and she gasped with shock as he backed her against the wall, his hands sliding the silver dress up her thighs.

His hand encountered bare, silken flesh all the way up to a pair of skimpy panties. In the grip of a fierce, primitive need, Nikos dispensed with this flimsy barrier with an uncharacteristic lack of subtlety, his entire focus channelled towards one thing alone. *Being inside her.* He touched her first, his fingers sliding deep, his breathing shallow as he gently tortured them both with this intimate prelude of what was to come.

She sobbed into his mouth, her pelvis moving against the stroke of his hand in an unspoken plea for more.

'*Theos mou*, you feel fantastic,' Nikos groaned hoarsely,

releasing the agonising throb of his erection before closing his hands round her trembling thighs and lifting her. His muscles were screaming with tension, every part of his body primed and ready for this woman.

He took her mouth again just seconds before he took her body.

Devoured by a primitive urgency to claim this woman, he thrust deep into her slick, quivering flesh, feeling her sweet tightness close around him like a velvet fist.

Intense pleasure shut down his mind.

He felt the bite of her nails through the fabric of his dress shirt. He felt the tension in her slim frame as she urged him to move—*urged him to release them both from this wickedly sensual torture*. But he'd anchored her hard and all the control was his.

He knew she was frantic. He could feel it in the tiny tremors that shook her, he could taste it in the soft sweet-ness of her mouth. He knew she was as desperate for release as he was. But for a moment—*just for a moment*—he held them there, the powerful force of their passion held ruthlessly in check while the sexual tension screamed between them.

Prolonging the moment, he withdrew slightly and drove into her again, and her whimper of desperation was almost animal in quality. She was trying to move her pelvis, her lips and tongue licking at his mouth as she begged him with every gasp and every trembling muscle in her over-excited body.

And he lost it.

Beyond rational thought, he drove into her, his passion an unstoppable force, his fingers biting into her soft flesh as he abandoned himself to the fierce burn of erotic sen-sation that exploded through his body.

The heat was incredible. She felt impossibly tight, her body closing around his, drawing him deeper, and he knew nothing except an explosive need to possess her in the most basic way possible.

It was primal, primitive—no finesse, no gentle seduction. He took her hard and fast, slaking his need with rhythmic force.

And when she came, he came too, the spasms of her body drawing him deeper until they were spinning together into a vortex of pleasure, both consumed by the same agonising starburst of ecstasy.

His final fluid thrust brought a shower of sensation that reached every single part of his body and his mouth was still on hers, savouring every single one of her agonised gasps.

As light gradually cooled the red-hot madness, he lifted his mouth from hers, his breathing uneven as he sought to replenish the oxygen levels in his starving brain.

Gently he withdrew from her body and lowered her. Her hands closed around his arms for support and he knew she was worried that her legs wouldn't hold her.

Unable to find the words in English, he said what he wanted to say in Greek, relieved that she couldn't understand him. Then he allowed her dress to slide back down her body and looked into her eyes.

Her small pink tongue moistened her swollen lips. 'So I guess the answer was a yes,' she said huskily, and he looked at her blankly, his mind still working at only a fraction of its normal speed.

She gave a slow, womanly smile. 'You liked the dress.'

Nikos gave an embarrassed laugh, shocked by the degree to which he'd lost control.

Never before…

Miraculously the exotic silver creation appeared to have survived such rough handling and his eyes dropped to her cleavage.

She gave a strangled laugh and pushed his chin up, forcing his eyes to meet hers. 'Should I wear a coat?' Her eyes and voice teased him. 'I think you'd better keep your eyes above my neckline this evening.'

Incredulous, Nikos lifted an eyebrow. 'You still want to go out?'

'Of course.' She gave him a little push. 'Nikos, I'm all dressed up. I have this fabulous dress that made you lose every last scrap of that iron self-control of yours. I want to wear it in public.'

'Why?' Hot jealousy poured through him at the thought of other men having the same opportunity to admire her body. 'We could have dinner here. We could stay in.'

'I want to walk down a red carpet.' Her hands on her hips, she adjusted the fall of the dress with a sensual movement of her hips that sent the blood rushing away from his brain to a completely different organ of his body.

'It's just a carpet,' he gritted, and she gave a light smile.

'Nikos, you were the one telling me that I need to enjoy myself.'

'We're too late.'

'No, we're not. Just give me five minutes in the bathroom.'

'Change the dress,' he growled, stabbing his fingers through his hair, his tension mounting at the thought of just how many men were going to be looking at her.

In less than five minutes she emerged from the palatial bathroom. Her tangled, ruined hairstyle had been redone in a more haphazard fashion by her own hands, but

somehow the lack of finesse made her seem sexier than
ever. Her mouth glistened from a fresh sweep of gloss and
her cheeks were pink from their love-making.

Nikos wanted to take her straight to bed.

And so would every other man who looked at her.

'Stop glaring.' Ella slid her arm through his. 'I'm going
to enjoy myself. Isn't that what you wanted?'

'What I want is for you to keep my ring on your
finger. Marry me,' he said roughly. 'You know it's the
right thing to do.'

She paused and lifted her eyes to his and he saw the uncertainty there. Uncertainty and something else.

Fear?

'You said you weren't going to mention it again.'

'Ella…' He felt frustration pour through him. 'After
what we just shared, how can you say no?'

'What we just shared was sex, Nikos.' She stepped away
from him, her eyes wary. 'I thought you said we're going
to be late.'

Never had Nikos been less enthusiastic about attending
a high-profile, red-carpet charity function. Instead, he was
gripped by a sudden urge to take her back to the canal boat
where their relationship had been insulated from the
outside world.

Cinderella, he thought dryly as they walked down the
red carpet a little while later, wishing he hadn't done quite
such an effective job in transforming her from shy nurse
to sexy socialite.

On the other hand, it was possible that the transforma-
tion would affect her in other ways.

Perhaps she would realise that they could be good together.

He watched as she smiled her way through a million

introductions, ate the banquet and danced until her feet ached.

He hadn't seen her so happy since those first few months they'd spent together, when their whole lives had been focused on their work and each other.

She sat by his side, her eyes wide as the charity auction started and some of the bids ran into the hundreds of thousands.

When one of the prizes was announced, she turned to him. 'Seven nights at the Mariakos Spa Hotel in Greece? Did you donate that prize?'

'Of course.'

Her eyes twinkled. 'So—if someone wants it, they just offer money, yes?'

'That's right.'

'And all the money goes to the charity, so it's for a good cause? Are you going to bid for something?'

'Of course.'

At that moment the huge screen at the back of the room flashed up pictures of the hotel. The camera lingered on an exclusive private villa within the extensive grounds of the hotel, an oasis of serene tranquillity opening onto a private infinity pool. The turquoise water appeared to blend with the sea beyond and there were a few wistful sighs in the room. A yacht sped across a sparkling sea, dolphins played in the blue depths of the bay and behind were mountains.

'I want to go there,' Ella whispered dreamily. 'I want you to bid for that.'

Nikos shot her an amused look. 'You want me to bid for a chance to stay in my own hotel?'

'Yes.' She gave him a pleading look. 'Can we? It looks fabulous. Is it smart?'

'Extremely exclusive,' he drawled, his mind thinking of a way in which he might be able to turn this to his advantage. 'Why not? A week of sun, sea and sex sounds good to me.'

Colour touched her cheeks and her glance was suddenly shy. 'I wouldn't be able to get the time off work.'

'Ella, you have been working without a break for the past four months,' he murmured, raising his hand to include himself in the bidding. 'You're due a holiday.'

'They won't be able to spare you.'

Indifferent to the fact that most of the room were looking at him as if he'd gone mad, Nikos raised his bid. 'I will find them a replacement. I have a friend working in London who owes me a favour. He might be able to step in.'

'Seriously?' Her face was alive with excitement. 'So we might be able to go some time?'

Bored with the game of bidding, Nikos offered an astronomical amount that drew gasps and then stunned silence from the audience.

'It's for a good cause,' he told Ella, lowering his head to plant a gentle kiss on her open mouth. 'So—we now have seven days staying in one of my own hotels. It will be an interesting experience. I've never actually stayed in one of my hotels as a guest before.'

Ella was giggling. 'I can't believe you just did that.' She leaned across and hugged him impulsively. 'Thank you. I'm so excited.'

As she pulled away, Nikos caught her face in his hands and stared into her eyes, trying to read her expression.

'Let's go back to the hotel,' he said huskily. 'I want you to myself.'

Within minutes of arriving back in the hotel they were in bed again and this time, as he dragged every last drop of response from her quivering body, he took her face in his hands.

'Marry me,' he demanded in a hoarse voice and she gave a moan, so shockingly aroused that she couldn't think straight.

'Don't do this to me, Nikos,' she gasped, 'not now. I just— I need— Please…'

It was a moment of exquisite intimacy, so intensely personal that there was nowhere for her to hide, and in that single moment as she lifted her dazed eyes to his Nikos gritted his teeth with the effort to hold back.

He lost the battle, his driving thrusts tipping her over the edge into an erotic sensual paradise, their passion carrying them along on a tidal wave of pure ecstasy.

Afterwards, he kissed her damp forehead and smoothed her tangled hair away from her face. 'Talk to me,' he murmured, and she gave a faint smile.

'You expect me to talk after that?' She pressed her lips to the base of his throat but he shifted away, wanting to look at her.

What was going on in her head?

Why was she still refusing him?

And when was she going to say what he wanted to hear?

Ella woke early the next morning, a feeling of dread in the pit of her stomach because she knew that tonight she'd be sleeping in the house again.

'What are you thinking?' Nikos asked, coming into the room, frowning down at her as she lay staring up at the ceiling.

'That I've really enjoyed this weekend,' she said softly. 'It felt as though— I don't know. We were somewhere else. It was good. What time do we have to leave?'

'Right now.' Nikos drew her up to him. 'We'll shower, change and then we can make an early start.'

And she was supposed to be pleased about that?

Feeling sicker by the minute, Ella followed him into the shower but this time when he made love to her, she started to cry.

'*Theos mou*, what is wrong?' Nikos switched off the shower and smoothed her damp hair away from her face with a gentle hand. 'Have I hurt you?'

'No, nothing like that.' She pressed her face against the hard muscle of his chest, feeling really stupid. 'It isn't you. It's me. I suppose I don't want to go home.'

He cleared the water from his eyes with the sweep of his hand and then lifted her chin, forcing her to look at him. 'We're not going home, *agape mou*. We're going to Greece.'

Ella stared at him, sure she must have misheard. 'How can we go to Greece?'

'You made me bid for a holiday, remember?'

'But not to go today.'

He shrugged. 'There is no time like the present. We both need some time alone together. So far our entire relationship has been conducted with the emergency department as a backdrop.' He gave a wry smile. 'I think it's time to think about romance, not resuscitation, don't you?'

'You can't be serious.' Stunned, Ella just gaped at him. 'Rose gave us the weekend off, not the whole week.'

'I have fixed everything. Stop worrying.'

Ella gave a disbelieving laugh. 'We're going to Greece for a week?'

Nikos reached for a towel and wrapped her up. 'Let's go. The sooner we arrive, the sooner you will stop repeating yourself.'

* * *

Ella lay on a sunlounger, staring at the still water of the infinity pool that appeared to blend seamlessly with the ocean beyond. The hot sun warmed everything it touched, from the bright green lizard basking on the low wall to the hazy peaks of the mountains behind her.

England seemed a million miles away.

'How are you feeling?' Nikos's smooth, dark tones interrupted her thoughts and she quickly picked up the book she'd abandoned.

'Fine. Apart from the shock of finding myself relaxing in Crete instead of racing around the emergency department. I can't quite believe I'm actually in your villa. I thought we were staying in the hotel.'

'I thought we deserved privacy, and it seemed ridiculous to stay in the hotel when my villa is lying empty.' He sat down next to her. 'Have you used sun cream?'

She nodded, acutely conscious of his spectacular physique. Every time she looked at him, her stomach curled with excitement and longing and she was mildly shocked by the effect he had on her. Would there ever come a time when he wouldn't have this effect on her?

'I love this place,' she said simply. 'How long have you owned it?'

'I bought it fifteen years ago.'

And she just knew. 'You bought it after your wife died.'

'Yes.'

'Did you live here with her?'

'No. We lived in Athens.' Nikos rose to his feet and she saw the tension in his broad shoulders.

'Sorry. I shouldn't have asked.'

'It's fine. And now I need to make some phone calls before dinner.' His tone was formal and distant. 'I'll see you later. If you need anything, just ask one of the staff.'

Ella watched him go, wishing she'd kept her mouth shut. Just a mention of his wife and he'd closed up.

Enjoying the peace and the warmth, she spent the rest of the afternoon lounging by the pool, doing absolutely nothing.

Nikos finally appeared when she'd showered and dressed for dinner.

'Are you ready?' He was wearing a casual shirt with a pair of lightweight tailored trousers and the ends of his hair were still damp.

'Are we going out?' Ella slipped her feet into a pair of pretty wedge sandals and picked up her bag. 'I assumed we were having dinner on the terrace.'

'Not tonight.' He held out his hand and led her towards the front entrance of the villa. 'We're having dinner with my family.'

'Oh.' Suffering from an acute attack of nerves, Ella glanced down at herself. 'What if I'm not what they want for you?'

'Stop worrying.'

He drove along dusty, winding roads, past olive groves and tiny secluded beaches until they reached a small village.

'Your parents live here?'

'My father was born here. He moved to Athens when he started the business and now he is semi-retired he divides his time between Athens and the island just over there…' Nikos inclined his head and Ella saw an island rising out of the sea.

'They live on an island?'

'It reduces his security bills,' Nikos said dryly, parking the car by the side of the road and leading her towards a sleek, expensive-looking motorboat that was moored by a jetty. 'Do you get seasick?'

'Ask me in five minutes,' Ella said faintly, allowing him

to help her into the boat and settling herself in the comfortable leather seat.

Nikos pulled up the anchor, started the engine and skilfully guided the boat into deeper water. Then he eased the throttle back and the boat picked up speed.

Ella laughed with delight as the speedboat bounced across the waves like a dolphin in a playful mood. With sea spray cooling her face and the wind in her hair she suddenly felt ridiculously light hearted. 'This is fantastic.' She turned to look at him, wondering what his colleagues would say if they could see him now. The Ice Doctor was no longer in evidence. He looked relaxed, bronzed and every inch the billionaire tycoon.

He may have rejected that lifestyle but, looking at him, no one would have been left in any doubt that he'd been born to it.

As they approached the island the water became shallow and Nikos steered the boat confidently alongside another small jetty.

A man and a woman were waiting hand in hand and the woman stepped forward and spoke in a torrent of Greek, tears in her eyes as she embraced first Nikos and then Ella.

Slightly startled, Ella assumed that this demonstrative exchange was a Greek custom. And then she felt the tightness and warmth of the hug and realised that this embrace had nothing to do with social convention. Drawn into the circle of the woman's arms, Ella felt that generous, welcoming hug unravel every cautionary layer she'd so carefully wrapped around herself. Without thinking, she found herself relaxing and tightening her arms in response.

The unconditional acceptance brought a lump to her

throat and when she was finally released, Ella didn't trust herself to speak.

When was the last time anyone had hugged her like that?

'This is my mother,' Nikos said gruffly, and Ella simply nodded, feeling foolish and yet at the same time comfortable because the woman still had a grip on her hand and that touch felt so natural.

Shyly, Ella greeted Nikos's father and then looked up in surprise as a horde of children came sprinting towards them.

'Nieces, nephews, cousins—my family is never-ending,' Nikos drawled, but she could tell from the sudden softening of his eyes just how much he loved them.

For the next twenty minutes she watched in stunned amazement as he shrugged off his cloak of icy indifference and opened himself up to his family. One by one, he scooped up his little nieces and nephews, while listening indulgently to a tirade of Greek from his father.

He responded with the occasional word, and then turned his attention back to his mother. As he hugged her again, Ella felt the lump in her throat grow larger.

How could she ever have thought him cold?

This man wasn't cold. He was guarded.

And she knew all about being guarded.

The family swarmed around Ella, asking endless questions, drawing her into their midst, until eventually Nikos took her hand in his and led her towards the house.

'My family are a little overwhelming.' There was wry humour in his eyes. 'I think you can probably understand now why I have my own villa, and why it is an hour from here. I made sure I was far enough away to make it inconvenient to drop in unannounced.'

'I think they're wonderful.'

His eyes lingered on her face. 'So why are you looking sad?'

'Not sad.' Just stunned, because she'd seen a different side of him. 'You have a lovely family. You're lucky.' *What would it have been like*, she wondered, *growing up knowing you were that loved?*

Nikos looked at her quizzically but, before he could respond, his mother descended on them and drew Ella onto a beautiful terrace that surrounded a breathtakingly beautiful infinity pool.

Unsure what to say, Ella glanced around her, feeling as though she was standing on a movie set. 'You have a beautiful home.'

'A beautiful home, yes. We are very fortunate.' Nikos's mother slipped her arm through Ella's. 'But a house is just a building, isn't it?' She glanced around the beautiful terrace, her gaze lingering on the orange trees planted in large terracotta urns and the brightly coloured bougainvillea spilling over whitewashed walls. 'What makes a house special is the people who live in it. And today I am a happy woman because I have my whole family around me.'

'I hope you don't mind me visiting,' Ella said awkwardly, slightly shocked to see that Nikos's mother was looking at her with tears in her eyes.

'Mind? It is because of you we are having this celebration. We had all given up hoping that Nikos would give his heart again. It has been so long.' She gave a slow shake of her head. 'The things I have read about him—the way he has lived his life—not good. Understandable, maybe, after everything he suffered, but not good. A Greek man should be settled with a woman. For all his cosmopolitan lifestyle, Nikos is a Greek man. He needs a wife and babies.'

Ella put her hand on her stomach, hideously embarrassed and self-conscious. 'He told you about the baby?'

'Of course.' The older woman looked delighted. 'And now we must plan the wedding. You must tell me what you have always dreamed of having and I will arrange it.'

Ella's eyes widened and she opened her mouth to say that they were still a long way from choosing wedding cakes when she saw the tears of joy in the other woman's eyes.

'Wedding? I haven't really thought that far,' she said lamely, but Nikos's mother pulled her into another tight embrace.

'You don't need to worry. I will do all the planning. It will be my gift to you.'

Nikos strolled across to them, a frown in his eyes. 'Don't put pressure on her.'

'Pressure?' Still holding Ella's hand, his mother gave him a disapproving look. 'You are the one who should have been putting the pressure, Nikos. This woman carries your child and she isn't even wearing an engagement ring! I can't believe a son of mine would behave like this. You should be ashamed of yourself!'

Nikos drew back his broad shoulders as if taking a blow, but he said nothing in his own defence.

Then he drew breath and his mouth tightened.

Sensing that he was about to divulge the true nature of their relationship, Ella reached out and took his hand. 'Nikos bought me a ring,' she said quickly, 'a beautiful ring, but it was too big for my finger so it is being adjusted as we speak. I think it's due to be delivered to the villa tonight. And as for the rest of it—we've been working so hard, this is the first break we've had. We haven't had time to think about a wedding. If you would help, that would be fabulous.'

Nikos stared down at her, his eyes blazing dark, his powerful body unusually still and tense.

Ella stood on tiptoe and kissed him and Nikos's mother gave a sigh of pleasure and delight.

'This is the best news I have had for a long time.' She clapped her hands. 'Celebrations. Time to eat.'

As everyone moved towards the loaded tables, Ella was enveloped by his family and for the rest of the evening she barely saw Nikos.

They were the warmest, most welcoming group of people she'd ever met, all of them insisting on speaking English so that she wouldn't feel left out.

By the time Nikos finally extracted her from two of his cousins and dragged her off to bed, Ella's head was buzzing.

'I love your family,' she said breathlessly as the door closed behind them. 'In fact, I love everything about this place. But I especially love your mother.'

The bedroom suite overlooked the pool and Nikos strode across the cool tiles to close the glass doors.

Only when he'd secured their privacy did he speak. 'Is that why you went along with her marriage plans?' His tone was harsh. 'Because you didn't know how to say no to her?'

Ella sank down onto the end of the huge bed, shocked by the chill in his voice. 'No.' Her heart was thudding. 'It wasn't. I—It just felt like the right thing. I want to marry you, Nikos. If it's what you want, too.'

'Suddenly it feels like the right thing?' His handsome face was devoid of expression. 'I've been asking you constantly. Why now?'

'Because now I know it's what I want.'

'You mean that having had a taste of the lifestyle that

serious wealth can buy, you think you'll enjoy being my wife?'

Ella felt the colour drain from her face.

'You know that isn't how it is.' Her hands shaking, she curled her fingers into the white bedspread. 'How can you say that to me? Why does it always come back to the money for you?'

His entire frame shimmering with tension, Nikos dragged his hands through his hair and muttered something in Greek. 'I'm sorry,' he said harshly, spreading his hands in a gesture of apology. 'I suppose I was surprised by your sudden change of heart. Given that nothing else has changed between us, it seemed like the most likely explanation.'

Ella stood up, trying to think beyond her bruised feelings. 'Or perhaps I just saw you with your family and realised what sort of person you are underneath that icy exterior.'

'What do you mean by that?'

'You love them, Nikos. It shows in the way you talk to your parents, the way you indulge your nieces and nephews. It's the first time I've ever seen you show warmth and affection.'

His eyes were hooded. 'I have been showing you affection continually for the past few weeks.'

'That isn't affection,' she croaked, 'that's sex. It's different. You keep yourself shut off. You don't confide in me—you never have. You've never told me anything about who you really are. But today I saw that you were capable of opening up. I'm absolutely sure you'll be a good father to the baby.'

He didn't love her, that was true, but she knew now that he was going to love his child.

And she wasn't going to deprive her child of that love.

He took her face in his hands, his eyes serious as they swept hers. Searching. 'You'll marry me?'

'If that's still what you want,' she said softly. 'Yes, I'll marry you.'

He lowered his head to hers and kissed her. 'Do you have any idea how long I've been waiting for you to say that?'

Ella closed her eyes, filled with happiness, sure that she was doing the right thing.

CHAPTER EIGHT

HER happiness lasted until they walked back into the house.

The moment the car pulled into the drive Ella felt dread building in the pit of her stomach.

'You're quiet.' Nikos switched off the engine and glanced at her. 'Tired?'

'Yes,' she lied, searching for a reason not to leave the car.

When she'd been in Greece, she'd felt as though she'd started to put her past and her fears behind her, but now she realised that it was all still there.

She glanced down at the diamond ring on her finger, hoping that it would give her courage, but the feeling of sickness intensified.

In Greece she'd felt optimistic and positive about the future.

Here, with the house frowning down on her, she realised that she'd been fooling herself—*seeing things the way she wanted to see them, not the way they were.*

Had he said 'I love you'?

No.

But that wasn't the biggest problem.

There was still so much she didn't know about him—

facets of his past that he refused to share. How had she managed to persuade herself that it didn't matter?

How could she risk her future knowing that he was withholding such a large part of himself?

'Do you want me to ring and say you can't work this afternoon? It was stupid of us to say that we'd work a late shift.'

'No. I want to work.'

Nikos frowned. 'If you're tired…'

'I'm not tired.' She didn't know what she was saying and she saw the question in his eyes.

'All right.' His tone mild, Nikos reached across and unfastened her seat belt. 'Shower, change, lunch. Then, if you're up to it, work.'

Ella sat rigid, unable to force her limbs to move.

'No,' she croaked, and he lifted an eyebrow.

'No to what? No to work?'

'No to marriage,' she whispered, emotion rushing towards her like a tidal wave. 'It's—I can't, Nikos. I'm sorry. I was wrong about everything. I thought we would be fine, but we won't be—It can't—Just forget it.' Mumbling incoherently, she yanked the ring off her finger, thrust it into his lap and then opened the car door before he could stop her.

Legs shaking, heart pumping, she tore down the drive, away from the house.

She didn't even know where she was going.

She just needed to get away.

'*Theos mou*…' Nikos was right behind her, his strong hands closing over her shoulders, stopping her flight and steadying her. 'What is the matter with you?'

'I can't marry you.' Her breath was coming in pants and she felt almost hysterical. 'I can't. I can't. I'm sorry. I made a mistake. I was wrong.'

'Ella—you're not making sense.' He gripped her arms tightly, his mouth set in a grim line. 'We have just had a great week together, you *chose* to wear my ring. What has changed?'

'Nothing. It's not you. It's me.' She covered her face with her hands and he gave a rough curse and pulled her against him, rubbing her back gently with his hands.

'You are very emotional and that's normal for a pregnant woman. You will lie down in the house this afternoon and I will explain to Rose—'

Ella drew away from him. 'No. I'm going to work now. I'll have a shower and change there. Don't try and stop me. I'll come and get my things later.'

Or maybe she'd just ask Helen to lend her something.

Nikos inhaled sharply. 'I don't understand what is going on here. What am I missing?'

Ella blinked back tears. 'Nothing.' She delved in her bag for her mobile phone, only to find that the battery was flat.

Nikos raised his eyes to heaven and produced his. 'Who did you want to call?' His clipped tone brought her even closer to tears.

'A taxi.'

'To go where?'

'The hospital.'

'You are planning to work in this state?'

'Yes.' Work meant not having to go into the house. And work usually provided a distraction. Hopefully, by the time her shift ended, she would have decided what to do.

'It hardly seems like a rational decision.'

'Just call me a taxi, Nikos.'

He pocketed the phone and pulled out his car keys. 'If

that's really what you want to do, then I'll give you a lift. But don't think this conversation is over, Ella.'

If she'd thought that a busy afternoon in the paediatric emergency department would take her mind off Nikos, she was wrong. Every case that came through the doors was challenging, serious and required his attention.

And all the time she was aware of his brooding expression and the rising tension between the two of them.

Why was life so complicated?

She couldn't just walk away—she was having his baby.

And yet how could she marry him?

Ella was checking the intubation tray in Resus when the doors opened and Nikos strode in. His skin had turned a rich brown after their week in the Mediterranean sun and he looked more handsome than ever before. 'The paramedics are bringing in a two-day-old baby with breathing problems.'

Was she the only one who was wishing to be back in Greece?

'Any more information than that?'

'No.' His eyes dropped to her mouth. 'And after this we're going back to the house. You owe me a conversation. Whatever was right in Greece can be right here.'

Feeling the sexual vibrations, Ella looked away. 'We can't talk about this now. We have a patient on the way in.' And she was already finding it difficult to concentrate.

'The sun has given you freckles.' He gently pushed a strand of hair out of her eyes, the gesture unmistakably affectionate.

Her heart gave an alarming lurch.

Why did he have to show affection now, when she was so confused?

Fortunately for her sanity the doors opened again and the paramedics hurried in with the baby and a very worried mother.

'He didn't wake up for a feed last night,' the woman told them, 'and when I looked in his cot he was this weird grey colour. I picked him up and he didn't cry or anything…'

The baby lay still on the trolley, struggling for breath, pale-skinned, displaying all the signs of shock.

A team of staff joined them and Nikos immediately took charge.

'Call the paediatric cardiologist and phone the neonatal intensive care unit and warn them he's going to be coming up to them. Ella, can you check his pulses? Brachial and femoral—I'm going to get a line in.'

Ella attached a pulse oximiter to the baby and then did as he asked. 'He has a very weak femoral pulse and his lower extremities are cool.' Which implied that insufficient blood was reaching the child's limbs. 'His sats have dropped, Nikos.'

'Check his blood pressure in both arms and both legs. And let's give him supplementary oxygen.' Nikos examined the baby swiftly, his hands skilled and confident as he searched for the cause of the problem.

'His blood pressure is lower in the legs than in the right arm.'

'Which confirms my suspicions. This baby has a coarctation of the aorta.' Nikos spoke in a calm voice. 'He's in shock because the ductus arteriosis has closed suddenly.'

'Do you want to do an echocardiogram?'

'Yes, but first I want to give him a prostaglandin infusion.'

'You're trying to reopen the ductus?' Ella prepared what

he needed and the team worked to stabilise the circulation with fluids and drugs.

'If necessary, we'll have to ventilate him.'

'Is he going to die?' The baby's mother covered her mouth with her hand, her eyes bright with tears. 'What are you doing to him?'

One of the other nurses drew her gently to one side but Nikos frowned slightly and indicated with his head that she was to bring the baby's mother closer.

'This is frightening for you, I know,' he said gently, 'but I am asking you to trust me. Tom has a narrowing of one of the blood vessels leading from his heart—that is why he is so poorly. He is not getting the oxygen he needs, but we have put in place a temporary solution. Come closer. You can hold his hand—that's good. Is there anyone you want to phone? Your partner?'

The woman's eyes filled and she shook her head. 'I'm on my own,' she muttered. 'This is just—well, you don't think it's going to happen to you, do you? When you have a baby you just assume that everything is going to be fine.'

Ella watched the woman close her fingers over the baby's tiny hand and wondered why it was that Nikos always knew instinctively what would help the relatives.

This mother needed to touch her baby.

'This problem with his heart.' The woman's eyes were fixed on her baby. 'Can you fix it?'

'My colleague will run some tests, take some pictures of the heart, using sound waves, possibly a few other things and then he will make a decision about how best to deal with it.' Nikos leaned across to adjust the flow of oxygen just as the paediatric team walked into the room.

They took over the care of the baby, but once Nikos

had handed over the case he drew the mother to one side, taking the time to explain exactly what was happening and why. He answered her questions with infinite patience, sometimes sketching a quick diagram to make his explanation clearer, occasionally referring to one of his colleagues.

When the baby was finally transferred, the mother was effusive in her thanks and obviously quite shocked by what had happened.

'That must be incredibly hard,' Ella said. 'Having a newborn baby and suddenly everything goes wrong.'

'And she had no support—that made it worse.' His eyes were on hers, cold and angry. 'Is that what you want? You want to do this on your own? Because you should know by now that that option isn't on my agenda.'

'Nikos—'

'It's time to go home. Get changed. I'll meet you by the car.'

Her heart felt as though it was being squeezed. 'I can't stay with you tonight, Nikos. I'm going to pick up my things and go and stay with Helen.'

'We'll talk about this at the house.' Without giving her a chance to argue, he strode from the room, leaving her staring after him in despair.

They arrived home at dusk and the moment Ella walked through the doors her mood changed. It was like putting on a heavy, dusty cloak, the weight of the past dragging her down.

The staff had already unpacked her bags so she had to pack them again.

'My mother called to ask your opinion on flowers.'

Nikos reached for his wineglass. 'I said you were tired and that you'd already gone to bed.'

'I'll call her tomorrow.' Ella stood in the opulent hallway, feeling sicker and sicker. 'I'll go and pack my things.'

But walking around the house simply made things worse. Every room she walked into mocked her until her head was ringing and she felt as though she was going mad.

She locked herself in the bathroom and splashed her face, trying desperately to pull herself together.

It was just a house, for goodness' sake. Walls, rooms, windows. Somehow over the years she'd managed to give it a personality.

It was ridiculous to allow it to get to her like this.

Cross with herself, she walked into the bedroom they were sharing.

It was a beautiful room, with a small balcony overlooking the beach and the deck. As she threw her belongings into her suitcase, she stooped to pick up a discarded shoe from the floor and noticed something sticking out of the bottom of one of the drawers. Assuming it was something she'd dropped, she picked it up.

It was a photograph, and Ella stared at it for a long, agonising moment before everything went black and she slid to the floor.

'She will be all right now.' The doctor closed his case. 'It isn't uncommon for pregnant women to faint. The baby's heartbeat is strong.'

'I'm fine, honestly.' Ella added her reassurance to that of the doctor, hoping that both he and Nikos would leave her alone. 'I'm just tired. I'm sorry to have worried everyone. I'll have a sleep and I'll be OK tomorrow.'

She really, really needed to be by herself.

But Nikos showed no signs of leaving. He spoke to his colleague and then asked one of the staff to show him out while he returned to Ella's bedside.

'You didn't need to call the doctor,' she murmured, closing her eyes and curling into a ball.

'Yes, I did. How did you think I felt when I found you in a heap on the floor?'

'Irritated?'

'Stop this. Ella—look at me.' His voice was infinitely gentle and she felt tears scald her eyelids.

'I just want to be on my own for a bit.' She kept her eyes tightly shut and then felt his hand slide through her hair, pushing it away from her face.

'I know you feel bad,' he said softly. 'I understand that. What I don't understand is why. And you're going to tell me.'

'Nikos—'

'Tell me what has upset you so much and we will deal with it.' His fingers gently massaged her forehead. 'I will do whatever it takes to make it better, you have my promise.'

His strength and kindness tipped her over the edge and a tear escaped from underneath her closed lids. 'This isn't something you can fix, Nikos. It isn't a noise in the dark, or a spider.'

He reached for something. 'You were holding this when I found you. It is a photograph of three people. A man, a woman and a little girl.' The hand that had been massaging her forehead gently wiped the tears from her cheek. 'Tell me who they are. I want to know why this picture has upset you so much.'

Ella lay for a moment feeling as vulnerable now as she had when she'd been eight years old.

She was painfully conscious of Nikos, his fingers moving gently over her head, infinitely patient as he waited.

'Tell me who is in the photograph and why seeing it upsets you. Is it you? Are you the little girl?'

The question destroyed all the barriers she'd erected around herself and she started to cry.

She heard Nikos say something in Greek, heard his stunned tone, and then the bed dipped under his weight and he was on the mattress beside her, pulling her into his arms.

'You accuse me of having secrets,' he muttered, 'but you are the one with the secrets, I think.' He didn't try and stop her crying, just held her tightly until eventually she was drained and exhausted with nothing left inside her except a feeling of emptiness and a pounding headache.

She lay limp against him, her head cradled against the protective strength of his body. 'I'm not the little girl in the photo,' she croaked. 'But I wanted to be. That's my dad and his wife. And the child is his daughter. His other daughter. She's the same age as me. They lived in this house.'

Nikos didn't loosen his hold. 'Your father remarried after your parents separated?'

'No. My father already had a family when he met my mother, but he didn't tell her. They had an affair. Mum became pregnant with me. For eight years he managed to run two families within ten miles of each other and no one ever suspected.' She sniffed and rubbed her palm over her wet cheeks. 'Do you have a tissue?'

He shifted slightly, yanked one from the box by the bed and wiped her face carefully. 'But he couldn't marry her because he was already married.

'I don't think he ever had any intention of marrying her. It was just an affair that went wrong. When he discovered Mum was pregnant, he set her up in a flat. He spent about half the week with us—the rest of the time Mum thought he was working. She trusted him. She didn't have any reason to doubt him. She thought he was wary of marriage. It didn't occur to her that he was already married.'

'He was spending the other half of the week with his wife?'

Ella took the tissue from him and blew her nose. 'I think that was what upset Mum the most when it all came out was that he couldn't even pretend that his marriage was empty and loveless. His daughter was exactly the same age as me. Draw your own conclusions.'

Nikos let out a slow breath. 'So how and when did you eventually find out the truth?'

'The cruellest way possible.' Ella scrunched the tissue into a ball and stared up at the ceiling. 'I was eight years old and playing in a netball match against another school. Suddenly, there was my Dad, watching. Only he wasn't watching *me*. He was watching a girl playing for the other side. He wouldn't have known I was going to be there because our school only stepped in at the last minute to replace the team that they'd been scheduled to play. I saw him standing there and then I heard the girl say, "That's my daddy," and at half-time she went bounding over to him and hugged him. I remember staring at them and then I ran over and said, "Why are you hugging my daddy?" and after that it's all a bit of a blur. I was…hysterical. They called my mum and it all unravelled from there.'

'And your father?'

'Well, he couldn't avoid it any longer so the whole sordid story came out. Lies, lies and more lies. Lies to both families. But his wife was willing to forgive him, providing he chose her. So that's what he did.' Ella gave a painful smile. 'He came into my room that night and said he wouldn't be seeing me any more but that he'd always love me. And that was it. He went.'

'He never saw you again?' Nikos sounded shocked and she shook her head.

'His wife threatened to end the marriage if he had any contact, and in the end they moved to Australia. But for a few months they still lived here, in this house. And I used to come here sometimes, just to see if I could catch a glimpse of him. I thought that if he saw me, he'd come back. I honestly couldn't believe he'd just leave me like that. You have to understand that I went from having a Dad who read to me at night and called me Princess, to this stranger who abandoned us.'

Nikos murmured something in Greek, scooped her into his arms and lifted her onto his lap. For a long time he just held her.

Ella sniffed. 'So now I suppose you're really angry that I didn't tell you.'

'I think you have one rule for me and one rule for yourself,' Nikos said dryly, 'but you're a woman, so that doesn't surprise me.'

She gave a choked laugh. 'The crazy thing is, part of me wanted to see this house. I always wondered what it was like inside. I thought seeing it might make me feel better.'

'Obviously it didn't. So now I am beginning to understand why you have been so reluctant to wear my ring. I brought you somewhere where all your fears were intensified. You are afraid of what I might be hiding, no? You are afraid that I will do the same thing to you that your father did to your mother.' His arms tightened around her and she buried her face in his shirt, breathing in his tantalising male smell.

'You had a whole secret life. You still do. There's so much you haven't told me. I suppose I learned at an early age that relationships are not always what they seem.'

'And sometimes they are exactly what they seem,' Nikos said firmly, tipping her off his lap and onto the bed so that he could pull his BlackBerry out of his pocket.

'Nikos?' Bemused, she stared at him as he keyed in a number. 'Who are you phoning?'

'My PA. The first thing to do is get you out of this house. I need her to make some arrangements so that I can concentrate on more important things.' He switched to Greek as the call was answered and Ella realised that up until that point she hadn't even known he had a PA.

As he dropped the phone back into his pocket, she stared at him. 'You have a full-time personal assistant? That's another thing I don't know about you.'

'I have two full-time personal assistants. They filter the majority of my corporate responsibility, leaving me free to practise medicine.' He pulled her gently to her feet. 'How are you feeling? Wobbly? Can you walk?'

'Of course I can walk. But where are we going? Nikos, it's dark. You can't find somewhere else to stay tonight. It's too late. Everywhere will be booked.'

As if to prove her wrong, his phone rang and he answered it with a grim sense of purpose.

Less than an hour later she was curled up in a deep, soft sofa in the penthouse suite of a boutique hotel along the coast. 'This is unbelievable. It's lucky that this room was vacant.'

Nikos shot her a curious look, seemed about to say something and then gave a brief shake of his head. 'We are lucky,' he agreed smoothly, 'that's true. Now—you are no longer in that place, I want to finish the conversation.' He poured her a drink of water and handed it to her. 'Why didn't you tell me about the house on the first day I took you there? You could have just said that you didn't want to live there.'

'No, I couldn't.' Ella curled her legs underneath her, feeling oddly vulnerable. 'I'm not a billionaire, Nikos! I can't just say to someone, "I don't want to live here, find somewhere else."' And, anyway, if I'd told you I didn't want to stay there, you would have wanted to know the reason. And I didn't want to talk about the reason.'

'If you had, we might have avoided a great deal of emotional trauma on both sides,' he drawled softly. 'Do me a favour from now on. Act like a typical woman and think aloud.'

'This is one thing I just don't talk about. I never have.' Ella leaned down and put her glass on the floor. 'It doesn't do a lot for your confidence, having your father walk out on you. You have to understand that my family was nothing like your family.'

Nikos ran his hand over the back of his neck. 'This is why you've been so reluctant to marry me?'

'I suppose it's all linked. You hid so much from me, Nikos—it just felt too much like something my father would have done. All those secrets. When I found out all those things about you it was a massive shock.'

'Ella—'

'And then when I found out that your wife and…about the accident…' She swallowed, struggling to put her feelings into words. 'I don't even want to bring the subject up because I know you don't want to talk about it with me. You don't share what you're feeling. You've switched yourself off, emotionally, and I understand that. You don't love me, so why would you talk to me?'

His dark brows met in a sharp frown. 'That is female logic. The fact that I don't spill my guts has nothing to do with my feelings for you. I don't choose to talk about the past, that's true. And clearly you are the same, *agape mou*, or we wouldn't be in this position now.'

'It really doesn't matter.' Ella focused on the picture hanging across from her. It was a modern seascape, painted in blues and whites. 'Feelings can't be forced.'

'You think I'm not capable of feeling?'

'I know you're capable of feeling,' she said softly, turning her head and looking at him. 'I just don't think you're capable of feeling the right way about me.'

For a moment their eyes held and then he sat down on the sofa next to her and took her hand in his.

'And it is my fault that you think that,' he said gruffly, 'because I have never given you reason to think differently.'

'I don't expect you to apologise for the way you feel—'

'You know *nothing* about the way I feel.' His voice was fierce and his hand tightened on hers. 'Nothing.'

Ella sat still, afraid to move. Afraid to speak—*unnerved by the depth of emotion she saw in his eyes.*

'I was eighteen when I met my wife. We had a wild, crazy affair. I thought I was in love with her—I thought she was in love with me.' He gave a bitter laugh. 'I was so arrogant back then, so sure of myself—of everything. I didn't think to question her motives. I married her against the advice of my parents but with the full blessing of hers.

They were delighted that their daughter had hit the jackpot. She didn't even wait for the ink to dry on the marriage certificate before she filed for divorce.'

Ella didn't know what to say so she just squeezed his hand gently in a gesture of sympathy.

'I would have given her a divorce,' Nikos muttered, 'because I knew by then it was a mistake. But I found out that she was pregnant. She'd tried to hide it from me—' He broke off and Ella slid her arms round him, suddenly understanding why he'd been so angry that she'd hidden the news of her own pregnancy.

'She was afraid you wouldn't give her a divorce?'

'Yes. And she was right.' His tone was harsh. 'I did refuse. We owed it to the child to try and make it work. So that's what I did. Unfortunately she didn't feel the same way. She was only interested in living a single life, backed up by the financial security of my money. I kept her with me until my daughter was six months old and then we had a terrible row. Awful. We were outside at the front of the house and she had Katerina strapped in the car, ready to take her to see her parents. She issued an ultimatum. I was to give her a divorce or she'd take the baby. It was the worst possible threat because we both knew she had no interest in the child.'

Ella sat still, horrified by what she was hearing and knowing that there was worse to come. 'I'm sorry,' she whispered, but it seemed as though he didn't even hear her.

'She was in a vicious mood,' he said thickly, 'and she drove away before I could stop her, with Katerina in the car. I followed her in my car, intending to take the child and let her go, but she wasn't concentrating and she lost control on a bend. They were both killed instantly. There was nothing I could do. I had all that money, but it was worth nothing when it came to saving my daughter.'

Ella's face was wet with tears. 'Nikos, I'm sorry...' Choked, she wrapped her arms around him tightly. 'I'm sorry you couldn't help her. You've saved so many lives, you've saved hundreds and hundreds of children—'

'I never want another parent to go through what I went through if it's within my power to prevent it,' he said bleakly, but his hand came up and rubbed the tears from her cheek. 'Don't cry. It was a long time ago.'

'But it's still with you.'

'Something like that is always with you. It shapes your behaviour. I learned not to fall in love with women. Love makes you blind. Love makes you see things you want to see.'

Ella swallowed. She knew all about that, didn't she?

'Well—I think I understand why you didn't tell me about the money.'

'You were different.' He spoke softly, his fingers still stroking her cheek gently. 'I always knew you were different. You were fantastic with the children at work. You were kind, generous—you were living on a shoestring budget but you always did the shopping and the cooking and you were always buying me little gifts.'

Ella blushed. 'Very embarrassing memory,' she muttered, 'given how wealthy you are.'

'I still have everything you ever gave me. A gift's value is not its price, but the sentiment with which it is given.'

'I'm glad you didn't apply that rule when you chose my diamond,' Ella joked weakly, relieved to see him smile.

'Which brings us back to the original subject. Our relationship.' His smile faded and he studied her face for a long, disturbing moment. 'So far we have stumbled along and made many mistakes. If I had known about your father, I would have understood why you were so anxious about marrying me.'

Ella gave a faltering smile. 'And if I'd known about your wife, I would have understood why you were so emotionally detached. So—where do we go from here?'

He lowered his head and kissed her gently. 'I still have to prove to you that our relationship is not about the baby,' he murmured against her lips. 'Ella, I would want to marry you even if there were no baby.'

She stilled, her eyes holding his. 'That isn't true,' she whispered, 'and I don't want there to be any lies between us.'

'It isn't a lie.'

'You ended our relationship.'

'Because I was afraid of what I was feeling for you.' His voice was low and urgent. 'Feelings that strong sometimes distort perception—I thought you loved me but I'd made that mistake before.'

'You left because you loved me?'

'Our relationship was becoming too intense.'

'You ended it by email.'

'You and I can't be in the same room and not make love, Ella,' he said dryly. 'If I'd ended it face to face, there would have been no ending. I needed to make you hate me.'

'I didn't hate you. I could never hate you. I guessed there was a lot going on under the surface but at the time I didn't know about the death of your wife.'

'The death of my wife is a constant reminder to me that emotions are not to be played with lightly.'

'When Helen wrote to you about the baby—'

'I was furious, but I was also relieved because it not only gave me an excuse to see you again, it gave me an excuse never to let you go.' He gave a shrug. 'I just hadn't banked on you refusing me. You are not good for my ego, *agape mou.*'

Ella made a sound somewhere between a laugh and a sob and buried her face in his shoulder. 'I love you. I really love you.'

'I know you do.' His hand stroked the back of her head. 'And I love you, too.'

Ella felt a rush of emotion. 'I can't believe you mean that.'

'Of course I mean that. Look at the evidence. I slept on a boat that is the same size as my car just so that I could be near you. I slept in your single bed and ate your cheese on toast—'

'At least you knew I was never after you for your money.' She sniffed and pulled away slightly. 'I'll sign a pre-nuptial agreement or whatever they're called—you know, those things that rich people always have so that their spouses can't divorce them for their money. I'd hate you to ever think that the money is the reason I'm marrying you.'

'And I'd hate you to think I might leave you, as your father did. That isn't going to happen. And that is why I have no intention of making you sign anything except our marriage certificate,' he drawled, his hand gentle as he slipped the diamond ring back onto her finger.

Ella stared at the ring, knowing that this time it was going to stay there for ever. She felt warm, loved, cherished and—*lucky*.

'I love you,' Nikos said huskily, 'and I know you love me.'

'I feel guilty that I made you move out of the house. What are we going to do now?'

'Right now?' He gave her a dangerous smile. 'I suggest we go and find the bedroom in this suite.'

She blushed. 'You're insatiable.'

'Where you are concerned, yes, that's true.' He delivered a lingering kiss to her mouth. 'I will never, ever have enough of you, *agape mou*. But to answer your question about what happens now—after I have spent the night showing you how much I love you, you are going to ring my mother and answer her questions about your choice of flowers for the wedding. Then you are going to choose the dress you want. And finally, *agape mou*, you are going to stand by my side and say "I do." How does that sound to you?'

Ella's heart melted with happiness. 'It sounds perfect,' she whispered. 'Absolutely perfect.'